Piers Anthony's eight books – *Chthon, Sos the Rope, Var the Stick, Neta the Sword, Omnivore, Orn, Macroscope* and *Prostho Plus* – have established him as a writer of great talent, on a par with the best of the new young generation of sf novelists. In an interview with the *Washington Post*, Arthur C. Clarke equated him with Delany and Algis Budrys. From the very first Mr. Anthony has been admired for his originality and inventiveness in both his serious sf tales and in his entertaining satirical novels.

D1435099

*Also by Piers Anthony and available
from Sphere Books*

MACROSCOPE

PROSTHO PLUS

Triple Détente

PIERS ANTHONY

SPHERE BOOKS LIMITED
30/32 Gray's Inn Road, London WC1X 8JL

CHAPTER

1

◆ ◆ ◆

Captain Henrys passed quietly through the interior lock and entered the barracks section. The off-shift was here, relaxing. They were sprawled on the bunks, some reading, some asleep, some writing fervent letters home. Several were talking in the passage between the lines of bunks, hunched over for privacy.

For an instant he felt a surge of resentment. In scant hours there would be success—or death. Yet here they were, loafing! But he caught himself knowing that they had to relax now if they were to be fit to fight then. His real ire stemmed from suppressed jealousy, for he could never ease off, and had no girl back home to dream of.

The sergeant of the hour spotted Henrys. "At ease!" he barked.

The chatter stopped immediately. Dice dropped to the floor and bounced as the nature of the huddle was betrayed. Henrys kept his eyes straight ahead, his signal that he hadn't caught anything illicit, and the men relaxed.

The sergeant stood up to report, but Henrys gestured him back. "Bruce," he said softly.

A young man jumped off his bunk and snapped to attention. "Sir?"

"Letter from Margie," Henrys said, putting his hand

inside his jacket. "Mailspec's on special assignment, so I'm passing 'em out myself."

Bruce hesitated only momentarily. "Gee, thanks, sir. I didn't know the mail was in." He stepped up to receive it.

But it was a blaster Henrys brought out, not a letter.

The crewman stopped, startled. "I don't understand, sir."

"I sincerely hope you don't," Henrys said. "If you move, you are dead."

The other men edged away, placing themselves out of the line of fire. "But what have I done?" Bruce asked plaintively.

Henrys' eyes never left him, and his weapon did not waver. "Tell him, Sergeant."

The sergeant looked grim. "Margie is another man's wife."

Bruce looked amazed. "You mean you'd shoot a man for a coincidence of names? Who else—?"

"*My* wife," the sergeant said. "Only Margie who writes here."

"But my girl is—"

"Your girl is Lucy," the sergeant said. "She hasn't written for a month, and it looks like a Dear John situation, which is why the subject hasn't come up recently. Maybe a lucky break, at that."

Bruce leaped—and the blaster fired. The crackle of lightning burst about his body, transfiguring him in midair. Then the corpse fell, smoking.

The men uncovered their ears and reopened their eyes. Henrys had paused just that fraction of a second necessary to give them that chance, for a blaster-bolt in closed quarters was hell on personnel. Now they crowded around, shaken.

The sergeant drew his knife. "Witnesses," he said.

Two of the dicers raised their hands. "Cap'n gave fair warning," one affirmed. " 'If you move, you are dead,' he said, those same words."

"And Bruce moved," the other said.

"And he booted the call," the sergeant added. "Legitimate suspicion, right?"

The others nodded tensely. The sergeant looked at Henrys. "Now, sir?"

"Yes." Henrys' lips were almost white.

The knife moved down and sliced into the charred arm of the dead man. The sergeant put muscle into it, cutting deeply, searching for an undamaged artery. He found it.

The blood that welled out was bright blue.

The crewmen began to mutter, letting their tension drain with the blood. The sergeant looked up, his face grim. "How did you know, sir? He had the rest of us fooled. . . ."

Henrys avoided answering. "I think this was the only one. But play it safe from now on. If any of you suspect a man you see is actually a Kazo infiltrator, cover him and bring him to me immediately. If he balks, scorch him. In front of witnesses, preferably!" He smiled briefly, acknowledging his own uncertainty, just resolved. "If someone mistakes *you* for a Kazo, you go with him, no argument. A little cut is better than a suicide."

"Sir," the sergeant said. He received the nod. "Suppose a Kazo covers up by drawing on a human? He could scorch the guy who maybe suspected him, then say it was a mistake."

"Good point," Henrys said. "Very well—I'll cut both parties—first the suspect, then the one who brings him in. And any man who scorches another will be cut himself—and scorched if he balks. OK?"

The men nodded. It was a grim prospect, but the situation required harsh measures, and they knew it. And they respected the man with the guts to do what was necessary.

Henrys held out his own arm. "So cut, Sergeant."

"Sir, I didn't mean—"

"Officers are suspect too. Cut."

The sergeant set down his blade. "Ecklund—clean knife."

The crewman named provided a new one. The sergeant

made a careful slice into the captain's exposed flesh. The blood that dripped was red.

"There's the precedent," the sergeant said. "You pass, Captain."

Henrys indicated the body. "Take it to the doc for autopsy." He turned about and left them, ignoring his arm.

Alone, he permitted himself a shudder. He *hadn't* known about Bruce. But he had heard wild stories about Kazo metamorphosis, and all officers had been briefed on identification procedure. Cutting was crude—but fast and sure, requiring no laboratory. Any delay in verification was intolerable; entire ships had been sabotaged by such infiltration. It was possible that some of the ships of this very Earth fleet were now under enemy control, waiting for battle. . . .

So he had assumed the worst, and reasoned it out: only certain crew members had been offship in the past month. If the Kazos were to infiltrate his own command, it would have to be through one of these. Seven, in all.

He cursed himself for not having checked earlier. What the men thought was an act of courage and discipline had actually been a desperation ploy. Sheer luck had brought him through the twin prospects for failure: overlooking a Kazo spy, or killing a human being. But he had been so busy with the preparations for this giant fleet rendezvous, getting his ship in order, memorizing combat formations . . . and, of course, every crewman had his clearance from the base hospital. No need to second-guess the medics . . . except that it was now apparent that the clearances could be forged. The infiltrator had gambled that no secondary check would be made, in the rush of fleet maneuvers—and had almost won.

But Captain Henrys made it a point to know every man in his command personally. When the dark suspicion had come to him, he had gone through the little list, checking each suspect out through simple conversation. He knew the minor gripes and problems, the names of the sisters and girlfriends, the childhood illnesses and fears, the verbal dialects and social ploys. John Dykes was certainly the same crewman he had known, and Arnold Cabber, and two more. He had about decided that his suspicion was paranoid, and was gratified that he had not made an open declaration of it. But because he always finished what he started, even when it seemed foolish, he had continued.

Now, carelessly, he had caught one. He had exposed the spy in public, forcing a showdown. The word would spread all over the ship in minutes, alerting any other spy that might be aboard. And two prospects remained to be checked. Bitool and Smith.

Henrys climbed to the null-grav tunnel that passed the full length of the ship. He boosted himself into a slow free-fall forward, then tuned out his surroundings while he pieced out the problem. He was being mooted as a hero, surely, but he had acted foolishly in two ways: by revealing his search prematurely, and by actually killing the alien. He should have been more subtle, not letting the creature know its identity was suspect—then capturing it bloodlessly for interrogation. A stun-beam would knock out a Kazo as readily as a man. So obvious, in retrospect!

That was a flaw he recognized in his own nature, a double flaw: carelessness and thoughtlessness unbefitting an officer of his rank. Unbefitting any man—for the same flaws had destroyed his marriage. But he would make the best of the situation—that was a strength in his nature, he trusted!—and see what benefit he might redeem from his error. There was a good chance that only one Kazo had infiltrated, in which case little had been lost. His chances of actually capturing a live Kazo and making it talk were minimal, as the creatures tended to go berserk when exposed. In any event, he could eliminate any doubt by arresting both remaining suspects and checking them physically. Kazos were blue, inside and out; if they impregnated their skins with human-color pigment, they still flowed blue within. One cut—

But they were warned, now. Any direct approach—surely they had bombs stashed away, or nerve gas, or perhaps wave-jammers. Any move on his part could be fatal to himself and the ship.

Yet he had to be certain. A momentous battle was shaping up—perhaps even that Ragnarok that would exterminate all civilization. He could not tolerate even the suspicion of Kazo infiltration aboard his vessel.

Maybe he had a chance, though. Obviously the aliens' purpose was not to incapacitate the ship early, for "Bruce" —he would have to message the command ship about that, and issue a general warning—Bruce had bided his time, not reacting until discovered. No—they would wait until it counted. Until his ship actually engaged a Kazo ship, or perhaps when the Earth fleet neared Kazo itself. Just as an Earth agent would do, to stop his home planet from being bombed. Even the increasing risk of exposure would not justify blowing cover prematurely. One ship was nothing; it was the fleet situation that counted.

He decided. He caught the handhold leading to the officers' deck and dropped to the floor, his weight manifesting as he picked up the rotation of the ship. Topside— actually the deep interior—was fractional gravity, but the outer shell was Earth norm, and therefore contained most of the working stations.

He strode into the command room and spoke into the general address mike: "Captain Henrys speaking. We have spotted and disarmed a Kazo infiltrator aboard the *Lliane*." Criminal euphemism? He had murdered the alien, not disarmed it! Why was he unable to speak the truth everyone knew? "The internal menace has been abated— but we are nearing the enemy sector of space, and the rendezvous may not be amicable. Alert status. Lieutenant Bitool to the command room."

In moments Bitool appeared. The captain stroked his square jaw with his left hand. His right was on the blaster concealed within his jacket. A blaster was a good weapon for use inside a ship, for it scorched personnel without ever puncturing the hull; still, he should have thought to pick up a stunner. The man did not *look* alien. . . .

"Lieutenant, you will be serving here in the control

room for the duration. But first fetch me the record on Smith."

Bitool nodded and left. Fetching files was the task of an enlisted orderly—but job and rank distinctions blurred in the course of battle duty. Strange name: Bitool. But naturally the potential alien infiltrator would choose a common one, like Bruce—or Smith.

Henrys ran his free hand through his straight black hair. How to play it? He did not want to kill again—but all too soon the fleet would make that fateful rendezvous with the Kazo fleet, and he could tolerate no traitor aboard. Yet if he challenged the man directly and happened to catch another spy ... ?

The lieutenant returned, carrying a small file folder. He was short—about five-six—and had a receding hairline. Kazos were that size, and bald. Bitool's fingers were quite long. Kazos had only three fingers, but they were completely limber, almost like tentacles. It should be easy to tell whetther two fingers of a seemingly human hand were artificial—but it was not. A man normally used only the thumb and forefinger separately, the remaining three digits acting together, except for such specialized skills as typing. But Henrys himself was a two-fingered typist, so that was no test for alien limitation. A Kazo could fashion a functioning human hand, and there really was no way to tell in the normal course.

Henrys did not look at the folder immediately. "I like to know my men as individuals," he murmured, sitting at the small map table and gesturing Bitool down opposite. "But you transferred in recently, and these are busy times. In this crisis I fear I have neglected you."

Bitool smiled, a little nervously. "I understand, sir. It's no piece of cake, this perimeter duty."

"Piece of cake?"

The lieutenant raised an eyebrow. "No easy job. The whole fleet is tense. And so am I."

"Yes, of course," Henrys agreed. He remembered the expression, but thought it had passed out of fashion a generation ago, at least. Which made it the kind of thing a

Kazo spy might have researched from a captured history text or period novel. On the other hand, slang wove in and out of the culture elusively, defying the inhibitions of the lexicographers, and this item could be in vogue again. It proved nothing.

"Is there something about Crewman Smith, sir?" Bitool inquired after a moment.

Henrys opened the folder. "There may be. He was granted planetary leave on a colony world three weeks ago."

"I remember. That was the same time I was transferred here to the *Lliane*. I rode the boarding shuttle up with him. Nice enough chap."

Chap. Dated, surely. Comtemporary crewmen were "slicks" or "zonks," depending on their experience. Not "chaps." But even if a spy's experience among men were limited to three weeks, he'd pick that up. Kazos were extremely apt at language, being able to master a competely alien system in a matter of days, including the nuances of dialect. So the spy would not be caught that way, and "chap" was probably a personal affectation of speech. Sometimes crewmen picked up dated slang from material in the ship's library, and sported it for a few days like a variant in uniform, to relieve the monotony.

"They're all nice," Henrys said. "When you know them. That's why it hurts so when they die."

"Sir?" Bitool seemed genuinely surprised.

"Didn't the grapevine catch you? Bruce."

"I'm not much for crew-gossip, sir. I don't have the rank to mix with the men without attrition of authority, and I'm still new to this ship. Accident?"

"Enemy casualty."

Bitool shook his head incomprehendingly. "I saw him this past mess, Captain. The *Lliane* has had no action in the interim." Then he did a double take. "The infiltrator you disarmed! Is that—?"

"The same. You did not see Bruce at mess. He died three days before you met him, on his own planetary leave."

"A Kazo! You captured it?"

"I killed it."

Bitool's shoulders dropped. "Thank God!"

The relief seemed genuine. Because the man feared any living enemy—or because a dead spy could not betray the living one? "It was murder," Henrys said. "They are living, conscious creatures, as we are; they have families at home that suffer as ours do. I do not thank my God for this act of mine; I shall do penance before Him for my folly."

"But a Kazo spy!"

"We are all God's creatures."

Bitool looked at him, face going blank. "Of course, sir. But war is war."

"Damn war to hell!" Henrys exploded. "It corrupts us all! Today I blasted a creature who was trying to save his world, when I would rather have been his friend, or at least made honest truce with him. War has made me less than a man."

There was a silence, during which the staccato of the fleet radio standby signal became loud. Then Bitool spoke again: "But how did you know?"

It took Henrys a moment to reconstruct the basis for the question. It would be about his discovery of the spy. "Process of elimination," he said, leafing through the folder. "No alien could have boarded my ship in space; the hull's electrified. It had to be by replacement of existent crewmen—and access to these is limited. So I checked out everyone who was offship in the past month."

"Why not for a longer period, sir? I should think—"

"There was a thorough physical a month ago. X-rays, blood samples—the entire complement was covered. It is not hard to spot a Kazo, medically; even a thermometer check will show that three-degree temperature elevation. Or a simple handshake."

"I have heard they can bring that down, temporarily," Bitool said. "They control heat dissipation by radiation . . . but I appreciate your point. Infiltration has to be recent. But what made you suspicious?"

"Just intuition. I wondered what I would do, if I were

the commander of the Kazo perimeter defense, anticipating an engagement with a fleet whose firepower was superior to mine. The answer was not difficult to fathom."

"Not at all!" Bitool agreed. "It would have been a bad show to enter battle with an alien saboteur aboard!"

Bad show. Dated, again. "No doubt. But we cannot afford to assume that the danger is past."

Bitool smiled easily. "Allow me to anticipate you, sir. The smart commander would not depend on a single infiltrator, would he? He would try to get at least two aboard, so that if one were discovered—"

Henrys nodded. "That was my thought, yes. It occurred to me that one should be a decoy, reasonably easy to spot. The other—"

"But as you said, Kazos are not difficult to identify—"

"Except when they are primed to berserk at the moment of exposure. Young Bruce leaped for me, and if I hadn't had him covered—"

The lieutenant considered. "Yes, I suppose that complicates it. But this is still no reason to tolerate infiltration by the enemy, who is surely not aboard to help your battle effort. Why not test the entire complement, right now, just to make certain?"

Henrys found his place in the folder. He set his finger on it, then looked up to meet Bitool's gaze. "Exposure means killing—we know that. I'm still shaky from the murder I committed half an hour ago. I ought to radio the fleet commander to advise him of discovery of the spy —but I afraid that would lead to much slaughter."

"But you can't keep silent!" Bitool cried. "Whole ships may have been incapacitated already, or even taken over by the enemy. If it comes to a fight in space—"

"I am aware of that risk. But I'd much rather *talk* with a Kazo, not fight him! And so would Earth's command. That's why we're on this mission! We have to be ready for battle, certainly—but if we can negotiate a truce between our species, and then a lasting peace—"

"How is real peace possible, when there can be no real

trust?" Bitool asked. "To the Kazos, men are vermin to be exterminated by any means—"

"That is heresy!" Henrys snapped. "If we delude ourselves about their very real concerns, they will delude themselves about ours. Isolation fosters suspicion. There must be a closer contact between Earth and Kazo, if only to dissipate such attitudes of ignorance."

Bitool backed off. "Yes, you're right! I apologize for my prejudice. But still, let me radio the warning—"

"No." Did the man realize that spies would intercept any such message, and be warned? "It could spread needless alarm."

"Needless? Let's assume there *is* another Kazo infiltrator. He could already have sabotaged the ship."

"Which means I can't afford to kill him," Henrys pointed out. "Not before I know for certain whether he has or has not planted a bomb—or done other mischief. And I can't just ask him, since exposure means—"

"Oh, surely the *real* spy—the one the decoy protects—would not be a berserker," Bitool said warmly. "As you pointed out, the Kazos must have sensible concerns, and are not ravening creatures of hate. He would have to be more intelligent, adaptable, able to assess his options. In fact, I should think his motives would be very similar to yours. What rational creature would choose devastating war in preference to honorable peace?"

"One who feared he could not trust his enemy?" the captain asked in return.

"Are the two species really enemies? Are *any* species of this galaxy, who have mastered space travel and all the pyramid of technology beneath it, really alien to each other? If only they knew each other directly, as one officer on a ship might know another, and comprehended how similar their motives were—surely space is big enough."

"To know each other like that—that would require a prior condition of peace," Henrys said.

Bitool sighed. "Is there no way out?"

Henrys looked down at the place his finger marked.

"Wallace Smith—treated two weeks ago for fungus rot on the left forearm."

"He must have picked it up during his leave. No crisis."

Henrys closed the file. "Are you familiar with the treatment for colony fungus rot?"

"Of course! I've had spots of it myself in the past. Takes about a week to manifest, after exposure, but then it's persistent. Only way to cure it for certain is to slice away the contaminated skin and destroy it. Uncomfortable, but necessary—and minor, when caught early."

Henrys nodded. "So Smith cannot be a Kazo. It would have shown up when the medic cut him."

"That's a relief to hear. How many suspects remain to be checked?"

"Just one, now."

Bitool paused, then smiled. "Sir, I rather like your manner, if it is not impertinent to say so."

"I like to know my men. You may speak freely."

"You are a forthright man, yet you appreciate the occasional need to be devious. I should think that if all men were like you, there would seldom be occasion for war. Anywhere."

Henrys shook his head. "Circumstance makes wars, not men. When the order comes, I shall do what is necessary, however distasteful I personally may find it."

"Circumstance," Bitool said musingly. "If it had not been for the alien menace, I would have mated. . . ."

Mated. Not married. Now Henrys was sure—and sure, too, that the usage was no slip. He faced a confessed Kazo.

"I was married," Henrys said, keeping both hands visible on the table. Bitool's own were there, too, the tips of the fingers almost touching his own. "But that same menace broke it up. I was at space too much. . . ."

The fleet receiver interrupted its staccato. "Henrys—pattern twenty-three." The bleep resumed.

Henrys kept his eyes on Bitool while his hand went to the ship intercom. "The alien fleet has been sighted," he said into the mike. "All hands to battle stations. We are assigned to escort the flagship for the conference, and it is possible that I shall be participating in the truce negotiations. This is a peace mission. Do not fire without word from Lieutenant Bitool or me." He continued with specific directions for other officers, so that the ship would assume it's appropriate position in the complex battle-ready formation that was pattern twenty-three.

At last he returned to Bitool, though his gaze had never wavered from the other. "They say absence makes the heart grow fonder—but she was a lusty woman. Humans do not always mate for life."

Bitool's eyes dropped. "Every four years the seaborn ones bloom, and the atmosphere is charged with a conducive fragrance. We contracted to merge at the height—but my call to service preempted romance. War before love. . . ."

"I am, I think, older than you," Henrys said. "Even allowing for certain distinctions in chronology and biology. I had time to marry—but she could not accompany me to space. I was gone as long as a year at a time—and one day I returned to discover it ended. My baby son was with her mother. I appraised the situation, and left him there, arranging a stipend for his care. I had hoped to remarry and make a proper home for him—but the so-called alien menace intruded."

"She waits for me yet, I know," Bitool said. "We do mate for life."

"Perhaps the two of us would have been better off with each's other's situations," Henrys murmured. "I would not have married, had I known—and you at least would have had a loyal family."

"Perhaps." Bitool made a peculiar gesture with his hand, as though some of the fingers were uncomfortable. "Captain—in the nature of things, one of us may not return to our planet. Possibly neither. This is not a proper query—but must the planetary antagonism, if it comes to war, be reflected in the personal?"

"That has never been my desire."

"If Earth should conquer—her name is Fomina, of the

Smiling Shellfish district, west continent. Tell her that Bitool passed honorably."

Henrys nodded. So the name had not even been changed for this alien mission! "My boy is Richard. Dick Henrys. He is eight—no, nine years old now, in Port York, America. I fear he is growing up wild. His grandmother is a stern woman—but he needs a father-figure, however distant. This war—"

"If you and I can reach accord, why shouldn't it be possible for our commanders to do the same?" Bitool asked. "I think I should trust you, Captain, to adhere to what might be agreed, in letter and spirit. There is no sabotage of the *Lliane,* and no bomb."

"I appreciate the information," Henrys said, meaning it. "Yet each must serve his own species first. When the interests of worlds conflict—"

"Surely war conflicts with the interests of each."

Henrys nodded again. "But the peoples of Earth have warred as long as war has been possible. It seems to be inherent. Even our courts of law arc in essence gladiatorial, with the aggrieved taking arms against the aggriever, figuratively."

"This is true with us, too. But when the armament of a single ship is capable of destroying all life on a planet —are there no reasonable limits to such a trial?"

"The fallacy of overkill has never inhibited man. If we have firepower sufficient to wipe out Earth eleven times, we deem ourselves losers. Against such lunacy, what chance has reason?"

"Reason is equated with treason," Bitool said. "Yet even the military must perceive folly at some point. We *are* the military!"

"Therein lies the faint hope of civilization."

"Why did you advise the crew to accept the order to commence fire from me?" Bitool asked after a moment. "You cannot know what my target might be! Your act seems nonsensical, in view of—"

Henrys sighed. "As we agreed: trust must begin *somewhere.* There is no risk I would not take, not excluding death or treason, in the interest of genuine peace. And this ship must have a captain, whatever develops. I may be required to transfer temporarily to the command ship, if the negotiations become complex and additional opinions are sought."

"Yet we both know that trust itself can be folly—"

"Greater folly than *dis*trust?"

Bitool spread his hands. "You have taught me something, Captain. I hope you do have occasion to make your own views felt. I shall not disappoint your trust, given occasion. But still I fear . . ."

"May our fears unite us!" Henrys said.

CHAPTER

2

◆ ◆ ◆

Dick Henrys and Jonathan Teller were playing tag along the paved alleys on the way home from school. Jon was a year older, and perhaps two years smarter—but his father, like Dick's, was a spaceman. This was a thing of mingled pride and loneliness, for neither boy saw his father more than a few weeks in a year, and less than ever now that the Kazo war was on. The other boys tended to exclude them, almost as if they were responsible for the alien threat. Not openly, because the two were smart, hard-hitting scrappers, but the onus was there.

Actually it was a more subtle, insidious thing. Dick's father was an officer, the captain of a ship, while Jon's was enlisted. But when either man came home he would take both boys out for a good time, seeing the shows and riding the rides that the maternal faction never permitted, and both would call him "Dad." Their philosophies were generally more liberal than those of the homeworlders; neither spaceman would condemn the aliens as evil. "They're just doing their thing, same as us," Spec Teller said. "They run a tight ship, defending their own," Captain Henrys agreed. This tolerance was reflected in their sons—but it sounded akin to treason to the fear-tight families of threatened Earth.

Once the two men happened to have overlapping leaves, for they were from different ships. Captain Henrys put on a civilian coat over the uniform he was required to wear at all times, so Jon's father wouldn't have to call him "sir," and they talked and joked as if they'd known each other from way back. They took the boys to the quarterly Victory Fair, and it seemed as if their roles were reversed. Henrys was a brawny man who knocked the bell in the mallet test, while Teller won them all free tickets to the girlie show by answering three difficult technical questions correctly without help. Then when the man made an age-challenge because of the boys, it was Henrys who turned back the lapel of his jacket to show the bright space eagle, shutting the man up. Dick didn't care much for the show, actually—he had heard it was the sort of work his mother had done—but he had a great time just going along, being one of two princes in the company of two kings. Hometime for spacemen was too precious to dissipate with military formalities or minor quibbles about age!

Dick was big for his age, and strong. He had almost closed the gap on Jon, physically, though the other was no weakling. Now as they ran, Dick was quick to catch his friend and tag him with a slap on the back that made Jon's yellow hair fly. They careened into a pile of metal refuse, sending cans and auto parts rolling. "Criminal waste!" Jon muttered breathlessly, kicking some of it back where it belonged. "We need this metal for ships, but the recycle detail doesn't even bother to pick it up, so it just clutters up the ground."

"Salvage isn't on the Top Ten priority list," Dick reminded him unnecessarily.

"Make no difference if it were," Jon replied hotly. "The politicos haven't cracked any real priorities in decades. Things just get worse and worse, and if the Kazos don't get us, our own garbage *will!* God, do we need a worldwide cleanup. Even the smell—"

"That reminds me," Dick broke in lightly. "C'mon! Grandma's baking today!"

Jon socked him on the shoulder. "Don't mention your grandma's baking in the same breath with garbage!"

Dick's grandmother—his mother's mother, not his father's mother (she was dead)—was an old-fashioned woman. She would use a strap on him when he misbehaved—a punishment he would not admit to anyone except Jon—but she also baked. It was as though the two abilities were linked: the chastisement of flesh and the kneading of dough. Dick knew of no other parent who could bake—not the way Grandma did, starting from scratch. The whole house would fill with the aroma of hot bread, and that compelling odor would waft out into the street, so good the mouth would water and the tongue lick the lips involuntarily. It was best when it was still hot, with the butter melting down into the ragged hunk.

So they ran toward Dick's home, happily. A light in the sky attracted Jon's attention, and he gestured, panting. "Ship coming in!"

Good news! Dick peered up beyond the skyline at the end of the alley, squinting. His eye for ships was dead accurate. "Fleet of 'em! But they're not on the schedule."

Now Jon stopped. They both had memorized the leave schedule, so as to know exactly when their dads would be home. This was the wrong day and the wrong month. "I never saw so many! Hey—*maybe the war's over!*"

The Dick's sharp vision gave the alarm. *"Those are alien ships!"*

Jon turned to him, stricken. "Oh, God—"

It was the end of the world. The Kazos had conquered.

All the tolerance for an honorable enemy evaporated. Dick had never doubted that Earth would prevail, proffering generous terms to the misguided and vanquished aliens. He had known the threat was worse than the government let on, but with men like his father defending, defeat was inconceivable. Now all that was shattered.

"Run!" Jon cried.

"But Grandma—and your ma!" Dick protested, for once more sensible than his friend.

Jon stopped. "You're right! We can't leave *them* and where else can we go? The whole world's caught!"

"An underground!" Dick cried. "We can hide, and shoot 'em from manholes, and sabotage their ships, and—"

"And they'll blast Earth to bits from space!" Jon finished. "Our fleet was our only real defense. Now we can't fight at all!"

"Maybe a secret force," Dick insisted. "Wait till they all come down, and think they're secure—then capture them all in one minute, and hold them hostage so the ships *can't* blast, then use their own ships to go after *their* world—"

"Forget it," Jon said bitterly, tears coursing down his cheeks.

Numbly they watched the ships descending. They were great ugly silent things, not fire-belchers like Earth's. They came rapidly, dropping behind the skyline toward the spaceport only minutes after the first sighting. No defensive missiles fired.

Jon shared his thought. "Shoot down one Kazo ship— and their dreadnought in space fires off a city-buster targeted right here. Same as we would, if we—we had—"

Then the enormity of it overwhelmed them both. Choke-throated, they heard the first conqueror ship set down on the concrete mat intended for the machines of human heroes of space. It was a full battle-wagon, not a shuttle; obviously the aliens were here to stay.

"Dad . . ." Dick said, unable to stop his own tears. For surely they were both orphans now. No man of Earth would have let the aliens through while he lived.

Now they heard a loudspeaker car cruising up the street. "REMAIN IN YOUR HOMES . . . OFFER NO RESISTANCE . . . CURFEW . . ."

Dick shuffled leadfooted to the end of the alley. He felt dizzy, and he put his hand on a dollar parking meter to steady himself as the car passed. "TUNE TO RADIO/TV FOR FURTHER INSTRUCTIONS—"

"Hey, kid!" the driver called suddenly, switching off the amplification. "Get on home! Curfew—they'll shoot anyone they find on the street after fifteen minutes! It's martial law!"

Dick turned a belligerently tearful face to him. "I'll take one with me!" he screamed. "A brick or something! "I'll—"

The car stopped. "The Kazos won't walk the streets, kid. Our own police are clearing the city. Because the ratio is a hundred thousand to one—that's *how many of us'll die for—*" He paused to flick back the loudspeaker switch, accidentally jogged on by a gesture. The accident would have been hilarious at another time. "For every Kazo that cops it!" he continued, unamplified. "You want to be responsible for a hundred thousand of your neighbors dead?"

Without waiting for an answer, the man drove on. His loudspeaker resumed: "NO HARM WILL COME IF THERE IS NO TROUBLE! REMAIN IN YOUR HOMES! THE KAZOS PROMISE AMNESTY TO ALL HUMAN BEINGS IF THERE IS NO RESISTANCE. CURFEW . . ."

"Come on!" Jon cried. "We *can't* fight! We have to go home."

Dick clung to the parking meter. "No!"

Jon looked at him understandingly. "Look—*they won.* We can't fight them now. If we get killed on the street it'll just make it even worse for our folks."

"They couldn't've beaten us!" Dick cried rebelliously. "They must've *cheated!*"

"Sure," Jon agreed, forgetting his own misery for the moment, in his need to get through to his friend. "They— they made a truce—and when our men were offguard—"

"Yeah!" But it was a bitter satisfaction.

"And we'll do the same to *them!*" Jon said earnestly. "But we have to wait till the time's right! Till they're offguard—"

Dick recognized the soft sell, for this had been his own idea a moment ago. Jon just wanted to keep him out of trouble until he cooled off some.

Two policemen appeared on the street.

"They're coming!" Jon whispered. "Run on home!" He took off, certain that Dick would follow.

But Dick would not. He clung to the meter, waiting to be shot. He wondered what it felt like to die.

They did not shoot him. The police understood, but they had to do what was necessary. The last thing Dick remembered was clinging to the metal stem of the meter before the big men in blue hauled him away.

CHAPTER
3

◆ ◆ ◆

The unfit perish, she thought, knowing herself to be unfit. She waited in line, hardly caring anymore. Her life had been bound to her fiancé; now that he was gone, she had no need to continue this anguished existence.

It was the dictum of the Conqueror that the population of the planet must be halved by the time of the next Seaborn Bloom. Control of live births and encouragement of suicides could have only limited effect in so short a span; there was no way to accomplish the complete reduction except systematic murder. Never in known history had an extermination program of such magnitude been contemplated. The inhabitants of the entire planet had been crudely ranked in descending order of fitness—by alien definitions—from the highly trained specialists down to the "surplus." Euthanasia eliminated that refuse—at the rate of six million lives per day.

It was her turn, already! Officials of her own kind, traitors for the sake of the fitness rating available, handled almost all of the appalling details. She would rather have had a Conqueror do it, so she could look him in the pale eye as he processed her for oblivion. Small consolation—yet better than seeing her own people perverted.

Two billion deaths a year—the stuff of those martyrs going to fertilizer so as to contaminate the living. . . .

26

"Identity?" the official said. There was not even any guilt in his manner, no emotion at all.

"I am better off than you," she said coldly, presenting her card. The Conqueror believed in numbers and cards; perhaps it made genocide less objectionable.

He put the identity under the scanner. "You are indeed," he said, surprised. "You have been excepted."

She stood there, her circulation missing its pace, making her hot and faint. It was as though she were a child again, learning to deal with the ugly shock of immersion in water. The properties of liquid differed substantially from those of air. She had been drawn out screaming, that first time, and suffered inclement visions even after she had mastered the medium. But this time she bore the shock in silence.

"Report to this address," the official said, giving her another card.

"But I don't mind dying!" she cried. "If I am spared, someone else will have to fill my fertilizer quota."

"True. But regulations must be followed. The Conqueror has removed you from surplus. Further debate will produce compulsion."

Hastily she stepped out of line. The alien rulers were merciless in their enforcement of regulations. She gave the official one more look of utter contempt and walked away.

Water had been a negative thing, turning positive only with time and experience. This was the opposite: a sudden, shocking reprieve. By this time she should have been free of her misery, her body already in the grinders. But the reprieve was at the behest of the Conqueror, which meant it was a negative development. And not merely because some other life would be extinguished in her stead. Yet she had to go, for there were worse things than the death of one.

The address was the private residence of a high Conqueror official. That meant she would after all face an alien. That brought her up short.

She knew herself to be an attractive example of her

species. The Conquerors had no females of their own. What duties were to be required of her?

She could die now, of course, not waiting for that.

No—there had been no genuine evidence of that sort of thing so far. The aliens were all celebate and not given to molesting the natives. The rumors were patently phony. Or so she had believed. Had to believe.

She swung up the trellis to the main windway and emitted her introductory scent. It was odd to find the invaders assuming native ways, but at least it facilitated communication.

In a moment an elder Conqueror appeared, much larger than a native male, whitish of skin and hairy of head. His cartilaginous nose projected from his face in front, his fleshy ears from the sides of his head, and great muscles flexed as he moved. She subdued her natural repulsion as she proffered her order-card.

He refused it. "Fomina, make of this shelter what you will," he said in a crude approximation of her people's etiquette. His accent was bad, but better than some she had heard on broadcasts. The aliens were very slow to learn native speech, yet they refused to make available their own language.

She was surprised at this greeting and not reassured. No Conqueror had treated her with anything approaching courtesy before, the few times she had encountered the species. But she replied in kind: "I will as you wish."

He put out his bony hand with its five hinged digits, and she forced herself to take it and to accompany him into the windway. His flesh was chill—several units below hers. Now she could pick up his body odor, acid and onorous. These creatures excreted some residues through their skin, so there was always an unsanitary aura about them.

A jar of fine mead nested in a holder, its bouquet streaming down the wind, relieving some of the stench. The Conqueror lifted it and poured some into a goblet, spilling a few drops. Fomina winced.

He gave it to her, incorrectly angled, and poured another for himself. She felt like an absolute traitor to her world, but she had to sip. Again she wondered why the aliens chose to emulate native manners. This one, this Conqueror Henrys, seemed to be making an extraordinary if misapplied effort.

"Fomina, I need your help," he said abruptly.

Her free hand went to her torso where the terminus nerve neared the surface, but she didn't quite touch it. The nerve was intended by nature to facilitate birthing, by prompting the expulsion of the entire contents of the abdominal region. Sharp pressure on it at other times could be fatal, as the digestive and circulatory apparatus normally occupied that region.

"I may have misstated my request," Conqueror Henrys said, making what she recognized as a gesture of conciliation. "I do not wish to affront or frighten you; you have nothing to fear from me."

"Then let me go," she said, surprised at her own temerity. This creature could have all her relatives to the fourth degree executed peremptorily if he even suspected disrespect on her part.

"I cannot release you, Fomina. You have been designated surplus, which means—"

"That I have no need of life. That is accurate."

He made the alien facial expression of discomfort. "Surely you cannot *want* to die!"

"Let me go."

"To do so would be to murder you. I cannot do that! Why do you oppose me, when I offer you life and comfort?"

She didn't atempt to explain. Six million Kazos a day. . . . Her horror was stifled only by her concern for her family, most of whose members were securely in the "useful" category. One word from this man could change that completely. But what he demanded was intolerable. "Let me go," she said once more.

"No!" he shouted.

This time her hand did touch the nerve. The Conqueror's bony limb shot out with awful speed and he grasped her wrist, preventing her. She felt the tension of those horrible muscles, pulling at tendons and bones, levering along his arm to exert cruel force on her. "I am trying to treat you fairly!" he cried. This episode was the first display of emotion she had witnessed in his species. "Why won't you at least cooperate?"

But she was beyond talking. Her worst suspicion had been realized and there was no further point in masquerade. Her fear-scent filled the house. If she died now, he might assume it was purely from confusion, and not take it as an insult. Her family might escape reprisal.

Henrys studied her, his round eyeballs moving gruesomely in their sockets. "There has to be a misunderstanding!" he said, still too loud, his accent worsening. "You Kazos don't suicide for nothing! You—oh-oh!" With that alien expletive he let her go, abruptly. "Fomina, *listen* to me! Hear me out, then do as you will. You thought I was suggesting—"

Again her hand went for the nerve.

"Bitool!" he cried.

It stopped her, as no other sound could.

"I know Bitool!" the Conqueror said rapidly, almost unintelligibly. "*Knew* him, I mean. He was in the Kazo intelligence service, and he infiltrated my ship. We talked—"

She could not move. Bitool! Her mate-to-be!

"He asked me to take care of you," Henrys continued. "It was a private pact between us. If Kazo won, he would see to the welfare of my son. But—" He stopped, seeming to want to say more, but unable. As though anything could be forbidden to the despoiler of a planet!

"Tell me of Bitool," she said. Dying would have to wait.

"I did not see him in his natural form. He was made up to resemble a human being—and an apt job it was! He passed as an officer of my ship for three weeks before the final encounter. But there was another infiltrator whom I caught, and that alerted me." He paused. "As you must know, your agents normally become aggressive when exposed. That way they either managed to disable the ship they were on, or to get killed themselves, so that interrogation was impossible."

"Bitool was no traitor!" she cried. "How could you talk to him?"

"Of course he was no traitor! We talked as equals, discussing the problem we faced—of war and killing. Bitool was not a normal agent, in that way. He was intelligent and sensible—"

"Yes . . ."

"He was a fine man, if I may use the term without prejudice, and I liked him. Our values were similar. So we agreed, as well as we could in that ugly situation. And that is why I put your identity on the exception list. I know he would have done the same for my son, if—"

There was no need to follow Bitool's career further. The fleet of Earth had won, and that of Kazo had been annihilated, obviously. Bitool, though prisoner, would have had to make a final effort—and if this man had slain him, that was part of war. She could not call Henrys murderer; not for that. At least it showed that Bitool had thought of her at the end. Now she could not die, for Bitool had risked his mission to enable her to live. He had wanted her to accept the protection of this particular alien—and Henrys was attempting to fulfill his part of the agreement. Still—

"If you have a son, you must have mated," she said.

"That is true. However—"

"Then you have no need of other—"

"No need at all!"

"Yet you said—"

"I said I needed your help. That—" He saw her reaction. "Wait, Fomina! Our conventions differ in many respects! What I meant was that I want you to be head-servant at this house. To maintain the premises—"

"Head-servant!" she said with immense relief. That would mean no threat to her family, and none to her.

"It is lowly," he said. "But I cannot otherwise authorize your exception. You are unattached, associated indirectly with the former Kazo military machine, and therefore rated unstable. Mandatory surplus category—unless there is specific need of your services. I delayed requisitioning a servant until—"

"Now I understand," she said. "I will maintain your domicile."

"I tried to phrase it euphemistically. I must have chosen inappropriate wording. What did I imply—in Kazo terms?"

She tried to demur. "It was a misunderstanding."

"Yes it was! And I want no further such confusions! That is why I need—I mean require the assistance of a native. It is too easy to generate awkward—well, like this one. I must learn exactly what went wrong."

It was best to answer. "An unattached female of my age best helps a male's need in a certain way," she said, trying to prevent her blue from deepening.

"That's what I thought, when I saw your reaction! But you almost pulled the plug before I could clarify the situation. It is vital that I learn enough of the native conventions so that I do not make similar mistakes in the future! Kazos may already have died needlessly because of our social ignorance."

"Yes. If you used that phrasing—"

"You must show me the Kazo ways. Call out the mistakes I am making, so I can deal with your people fairly."

"Why should it matter to you?" she asked. "The Conqueror sets the standards; our opinions mean nothing."

"It *does* matter! We have established the overall guidelines—but we are largely dependent on native assistance to implement our programs. If we allow ourselves to be ignorant, corruption becomes possible at the native level. The families of our native aides may be spared, their places taken by genuinely fit families who do not accede to the graft. This would be an intolerable perversion of our program. But if we learn the native ways well enough to perceive—"

That made sense, for there *was* a certain amount of favoritism shown to the families of Kazo collaborators. It seemed that not all the evils of the system stemmed from the will of the Conqueror! But was he sincere? It was best to know immediately.

"There are a number of errors," she said. "Your protocol of entry is a parody—and your mead should be placed upwind, for the bouquet to pass all through the house—and you must never spill the mead when serving, for that means you do not value the esteem of your guest—"

"That's it exactly!" he exclaimed.

"And you must not raise your voice, for that signifies hostility. If your actual words are mild or complimentary, volume renders them sarcastic."

"Oh," he said, much more softly. "All the things you know—you must teach me. This is what I most need—require, ask, wish—"

"Prefer," she said. "Preference has no onus; need *does*. Also, you should not address a female by her complete name. I am called Fomin by those outside my family, and undue familiarity—"

"I can see our attempts to conform to your customs have been a webwork of insult," Henrys said.

"We assumed it was intentional," she said. "Perpetual mocking of our ways, showing contempt. Phrases like 'pull the plug . . .' even your smell—"

"Smell?"

"Were you not aware that the odors of your bodies are disgusting to us?"

"No. But we shall work on that!"

Nothing she said seemed to insult him. He *was* sincere —or impervious to social affront. "You are the Conqueror," she said. "We all hate you. Nothing but your absence can change that. Even if fairly administered, your policies are genocidal! Why should you try to conform to our conventions, then?"

"Golden rule," he said. "We try to treat you as we would have you treat *us*—were the situation reversed."

Typical Conqueror logic! Her people were being systematically decimated—but he wanted to honor their household etiquette! As though manners could compensate for murder.

Yet she had to serve him. This Conqueror Henrys was her closest link to her lost beloved, Bitool.

"In time perhaps you will better appreciate our motives," he said. "We are not really barbarians. We are trying to help you in ways you cannot help yourselves. Even the assigned 'surplus' is merely the equivalent of nature's way—the survival of the fittest."

"And you would have *us* slaughter *your* millions—if we ruled you," she said, disbelievingly. "And your widows would serve our males."

"I don't expect you to accept this," he said. "But the answer is yes." He paused. "I cannot tell you what happened in space, except this much: I did not kill Bitool. You will not see him again—but the agreement he and I made was never voided."

Was that supposed to represent some consolation? She wasn't sure.

She could have poisoned him, as he permitted her to shop in the local markets unsupervised, and he ate what she prepared. Conqueror Henrys was determined to go native in dress, diet, and manner. He accompanied her to Kazo cultural programs and he mixed freely with the Kazo populace, always asking questions, always listening to the answers. He had to undertake a harsh regimen of cleaning and medication to abate the Conqueror odors, but he could keep it down for an hour or more. He talked with Kazo intellectuals, and admitted his errors in perception and logic. The relationship between the two species was one of cordial hate, and he never pretended otherwise—but she perceived a steady shift in the attitude of those he dealt with, the hate becoming less certain, the respect greater.

Small changes began to appear in Conqueror policy, obviously stemming from this continuous quest for knowledge. Certain native administrators became surplus, and certain surplus Kazos became officially fit. Corruption became increasingly hazardous to its practitioners.

All Kazos longed for a day of retaliation. All knew it

was futile; the Conqueror had too much power, and was too ruthless in its application, and too perceptive in fathoming counterplots. Still the vision expanded, with an entire mythology supporting it. Part of that myth concerned a lone Kind Conqueror, who tried to mitigate the onus, who addressed Kazos as equals, yet without apology for his position. On the day of reckoning, that one alien would not be slain.

Henrys was a mature man, dedicated and honest. There was that in him that resembled Bitool. Fomina told herself that she respected his sincerity, and that she needed to cultivate him for the sake of the small reforms that resulted in Conqueror policy, and that he remained her only link with her dead beloved. But gradually she knew that it was more than that.

She was moving into an emotional attachment to an alien creature. And that was inconceivable.

She should have poisoned him, for he represented more than the force that was slaughtering her people at the rate of millions a day. He represented the transposition of Kazo hate into a certain dubious Kazo respect, and that would slide on into eventual acceptance of Conqueror rule. Already there were those who whispered that the world was better off with the easing of severe population pressure and conservation of resources. In time the myth of reckoning would be dominated by the myth of the Kind Conqueror—and then it really would be mythological.

But she could not bring herself to do her duty to her people.

It was a girl, hardly ten years old, running furtively from house to house. A police vehicle was after her, sniffing out her trail relentlessly; the alien siren was plainly audible.

Grime spattered the fugitive's blue head, giving her the grotesque appearance of Conqueror-type hair. Her breath rasped out of her nose-concavity. Yet she was a pretty child, alert and well-formed. Obviously newly-surplus.

Fomina set down her basket of wind-dried smocks.

Her eye caught that of the girl. The wind carried her come-to-me scent to the other.

They scrambled up the trellis and into the windway. "But I can't hide *here!*" the child cried, recognizing the domicile of a Conqueror.

"You can't hide *anywhere!*" Fomina replied. "There is only one chance. If you can obtain an exception—" She went to Henrys' office.

The Conqueror turned from his viewer. He spent many hours a day going over papers: records, specifications, reports. The child saw him and screamed, thinking herself betrayed, but Fomina held her in place.

"What is it, Fomin?" Henrys inquired, as if this were nothing out of the ordinary. He wore glasses now: matched lenses of glass that enhanced his alien demeanor.

"The police are after this poor child!" Fomina said. "I could not let her die!"

Henrys frowned, well understanding the nature of her request. "I cannot intercede in a matter of law. But perhaps this is a confusion. Who are you, child?"

"Tell him the truth!" Fomina said before the child could speak. "He can read your scent as a Kazo would."

The child slumped, her prevarication odor fading. "Serena. My family was just declared surplus. I ran."

Henrys punched buttons on his viewer, and words rippled across it. "Your parents found each other incompatible. They attempted asocial behavior. Is that a true specification?"

"Yes . . ." the child said.

"On Earth we would call that divorce, and it would not be the occasion for a verdict of surplus," Henrys said. "Otherwise I myself would be dispatched. . . ."

For a moment Fomina dared to hope.

"But here on Kazo, by the decree of your own people, such behavior is intolerable," Henrys said "This is as it should be. There is no fit home for this child."

"But she is blameless!" Fomina protested.

"It is not always possible to separate the innocent from the guilty," he said. "You yourself were blameless, Fomin."

She had no answer to that. A child bereft of family was obviously surplus.

"Seren," Henrys asked gently, "do you really wish to survive your parents?"

The child collapsed, shuddering. It ripped something out of Fomina. "Conqueror, everything else you do I can comprehend. But this continual murder—how can you do it? Spare her family—for her sake!"

Now the police vehicle was outside. Henrys turned a knob on his viewer, and the scene shifted to the Kazo official. "She is here," Henrys said.

"At least investigate!" Fomina cried. "It cannot have been a deeply rooted incompatibility! This child has had good upbringing! Look at her clothing, her health, her grief!"

But Serena's clothing was dirty and torn from the chase, and her grief could be for herself.

The Kazo's face on the screen was respectful. "Are you interceding, Conqueror?"

"No."

"But they will grind her up!" Fomina cried. "This victim of circumstance—"

Henrys sighed. "Fomin, the population must be halved, and we are not yet near the target. There is no kind way to do it, only rigorous adherence to standards set up objectively. Only when the sheer numbers fall within the guideline can this policy be mitigated. The potential replenishment of planetary resources must match the potential depletion. Otherwise a much crueler fate awaits your people: starvation, illness, and anarchy. We must kill selectively today so that your people will live tomorrow, freed from genetic liabilities and debilitating illnesses. We cannot afford arbitrary exceptions, for that is the beginning of corruption. If this child should live, another would have to die—either by our hand or by the stresses of the situation. There is no choice."

And it was true. The figures did not lie, for the Kazo had known it before the Conqueror came. The pressure of population against diminishing resources was irresistible, and the standard of living had been declining for decades. But no faction had been able to take the initiative that everyone knew was necessary—until the Conqueror had done it for them, brutally but effectively.

Henrys would not bend. He *could* not. He was saving a world by executing its surplus population, and he knew that any corruption of that principle would lead inevitably to failure of the entire mission.

Fomina knew all this. But the logic of murder conflicted irreconcilably with the needs of the individual. If salvation of the species meant the butchery of this terrified child—was the species worth saving? Fomina herself had been excepted through Henrys' intercession; was this the life that was being taken in lieu of hers?

Henrys charged from his seat toward her, but too late. Fomina had reached the nerve before being aware of it herself, and collapsed in a birthing of blue blood.

"Why?" the Conqueror cried in alien anguish that seemed so strongly akin to her own. "Fomin—Fomina— you *understood*—"

"I know you will do what is right," she said. She fought to hold back the other thing, but it burst out unbidden. "I love—"

Then the blood flowed out from her brain, and she thought she saw Bitool.

CHAPTER

4

◇ ◇ ◇

If Bitool really wanted a favor, he had chosen a remarkably inappropriate occasion to make his desire known. Yet he stood at ease, one blue hand resting lightly upon the stolid desk, the press of his conservative business suit undisturbed. His nose and ears were so similar to the human equivalent that the Earthman was sure they were artificial appendages. The eyes and mouth deviated more, so were probably unaltered. Bitool was, every inch, every nuance, the genteel alien executive.

"Let's not play at formalities," Dick Henrys said. "You know I am your enemy." But the words emerged awkwardly; he felt like a sophomore prankster standing before the dean.

The Kazo overlord of North-Central America smiled, conveying in a single expression both the humor of his spirit and the clockwork calculation of his brain. "I do need your assistance," he said. "As you are a man of courage and honor, I am asking you to make your decision at this moment."

"Honor!" Henrys looked around the austere office, unable to meet the overlord's gaze. "I came here to kill you, and you are offering me my freedom—in exchange for just three days of service? With a revolution breaking over your head?"

Bitool's manner changed. He snapped all three fingers imperatively. "Immediate response, Earthman: what is a revolutionist?"

"A revolutionist is one who desires to discard the existing social order and try another."

Bitool snapped his fingers again, ringingly. Those tentacular appendages were very good at that! "Under what circumstances is a man a revolutionist?"

"Every man is a revolutionist concerning the thing he understands."

Snap! "And what oppression has revolution eased?"

"Revolutions have never lightened the burden of tyranny; they have only shifted it to another shoulder."

Bitool smiled again. "Please pick up the volume beside you, Richard."

Henrys glanced at the table on his right and found a slim book there. He reached for it.

"Identify it, Richard." Smile without snap.

He read from the title page: *"The Revolutionist's Handbook and Pocket Companion,* by John Tanner, M.I.R.C."

"Keep it, Richard. You will find its contents revealing." The overlord's expression became enigmatic, even for an alien. "But now you must give me your commitment. I must have your cooperation during the crisis."

Henrys studied him, searching for some clue to his intent. The Kazo now puffed a local cigar. His blue face and hands were distinctly foreign, but nothing else was. He looked, as he stood, as much like a human being as an Extraterrestrial being.

"I don't see how you could afford to take my word for such a thing," Henrys said at last, "or how I could give it. It is better for me to die than to turn against my cause." Why did his words sound so much like an inept reading? He believed what he said. . . .

"You will not be required to betray any confidences. You would not be traitor to your principles."

"But why won't you tell me in advance what you want me to do?"

"You may need your weapon," Bitool said. His arm moved, and suddenly the tiny round palm-pistol Henrys had brought was in the air.

Henrys caught it automatically, his free hand circling it and positioning the stubby muzzle before his mind reacted to the surprise of the gesture. "You disarmed it, of course," he said. He aimed at the hanging light fixture and squeezed the bulb.

A puff of gas appeared and dissipated as the weapon kicked his hand. Glass exploded as the ball-shot struck its mark. The bitter odor of the expended round tugged momentarily at his nostrils.

Bitool stood calmly, watching him with a peculiar understanding.

Henrys looked at the cooling pistol, astonished. "I can kill you," he said. "You aren't using a projectile-shield, and you're too far away to disarm me with that trick motion you used before."

"You must decide."

Henrys aimed at him. "Do you *want* to die?"

"You are very like your father," Bitool said.

Something flared in Henrys' mind, at once nostalgic and awful. He fought for control, knowing the overlord was attempting to play upon his emotional responses just as he had upon his intellectual ones.

Earth was under the blue heel of the alien—conquered more readily than the cheapest pulps had predicted. He had wondered many times what had become of the valiant resistance, the desperate last-ditch heroics supposed to make his planet a savagely expensive property for any invader.

Man had anticipated nightmarish, monstrous slimy slugs, or hairy man-sized telepathic centipedes, or metallic animate boxes with carnivorous appetites. Such a demise would at least have had the dignity of horror. But to have submitted without opposition to moderately sized blue humanoids, so close in form to man that half an hour with a makeup artist could make them pass—

The Kazos had conquered without apparent effort,

and their rule was skilled and stern—yet in the long view, benign. It was difficult even to hate them properly, despite the fantastic massacre they had overseen on Earth.

It did not add up. There were histories of the Kazo peoples in the Earth libraries now. Henrys had taken pains to study them, and had discovered no supermen therein. The Kazos had warred and struggled for civilization in a manner so similar to that of man that the texts seemed phony: thinly concealed allegories of Earth, published to conceal the aliens' true nature and intent.

The Kazos were *good* administrators. If they had warred as blindly as they seemed to want men to believe, and done it throughout their development, how had they been so abruptly transformed into superlative administrators and unflinching enforcers? Granted that they had their great ones, as did mankind, what alchemy brought *only* this type to captive Earth? In the normal course the surplus of their crowded planet should have emigrated to the planet being readied for occupation, not just these few chosen males.

You are very like your father. . . . What did Bitool know of Captain Henrys, dead from the date of the Conquest? Nothing, obviously.

Now the leading Kazo of the area was bluffing with his own life. Yet Bitool was no fool. Better to spring the trap immediately, rather than to allow himself to be maneuvered into betrayal of his people.

"You're forcing me to join you—or to kill you," Henrys said. "You think this will make me believe you. This practical gesture of trust."

" 'Beware of the man whose god is in the skies,' " the overlord said calmly.

It was a quotation, and the note was false. "I *don't* believe you." Henrys squeezed the bulb.

The shot smacked into the wall beside the Kazo's head. Angry, Henrys squeezed again—and missed on the other side. Bitool had not moved.

Henrys stared at his hand, knowing it had disobeyed him. He was a dead shot with this weapon, but his body had obeyed a will deeper than his conscious one, making him unable to aim directly at the overlord and fire.

"I *do* believe you," he said, defeated.

Bitool turned. "Come, Richard," he said gently. "Your god is not in the skies. You shall be the first human to see."

Henrys followed him, realizing that he had been committed. He slipped the book into his shirt and the pistol into his pocket. Why had he shied away from the execution that had been his assignment?

They took the private lift reserved for the overlord—one of the few privileges the conqueror claimed—and plummeted to the ground floor. They left the administration building together, as though they were friends. Bitool elected to walk instead of summoning a car or descending to the public conveyors one and two levels below.

Here the life of the city continued pretty much as it always had: electric cars rolled along the measured lanes and pedestrians crowded the sidewalks. On this level alone the two could meet: antique flashing lights required the vehicles to halt periodically to let the walkers cross.

It was inefficient, but Henrys loved it. Most of the city and most of the world reflected the phenomenal decline in population, so that there was little actual crowding. But selected levels had been preserved intact, and the flavor of pre-Kazo life remained.

Henrys had spent the past two years in the Survey Department, charting this level: traffic flow, residential density, patterns of industry and employment. He knew almost every aspect of this cross-section of the city—and very little of the levels above and below, the changed ones. It was all part of some nebulous Kazo project: perhaps they meant to reorganize this antique layer too. The overlords never acted without complete information.

Bitool was shorter and lighter than most of the people on the walk, but he seemed completely at ease. No guards challenged them in the clamorous shopping area. No one paid attention to the Extraterrestrial creature walking among them on this conventional American city street. Of course the Kazos themselves had decreed that they were to be ignored unless they took the initiative—but even so, there should have been surreptitious glances. It occurred to Henrys that he had never seen a Kazo with a bodyguard.

At the first corner a mother was trying ineffectively to keep her small child reined while carrying a heavy package of groceries. Henrys wondered idly how she would have done in the time before the limit of one baby per couple had been imposed.

Bitool stopped and bowed. "Please," he murmured, taking the package in one hand and catching the little boy's arm with the other. The lady blushed, flattered, while Henrys averted his face in disgust. A human woman!

Bitool escorted her across the street, then returned child and package and bowed farewell. Henrys was conscious of the woman's gaze as they walked away. It had not occurred to him to assist her, and Bitool's action astonished him. Why such artificial chivalry in the alien conqueror?

Yet the woman had seemed pleased. She should have recoiled from the physical touch of the deep blue hand taking her package, and clutched her child instinctively away from that three-fingered contact, reacting as she would against the touch of the scales of a python. The child should have screamed.

Their pleasure could not have been servile appeasement. No Kazo had ever expressed sexual interest in an Earthwoman, and there was a general suspicion that the aliens were in fact neuter, despite plain statements to the contrary in the alleged histories. Certainly only one sex had come to Earth, and if there was miscegenation it was a complete secret.

Henrys found his mind unusually active as he accompanied Bitool on the brisk hike. There were other mysteries about the Conquest. How had Earth been subdued, and how had pacification been maintained? There had been scattered resistance at first, as there had to be despite the real threat of retaliation, but it had quickly faded. The current revolution was the first he had direct knowledge of in a dozen years. Even allowing for suppression of the press—though it did not *seem* suppressed—this was hardly credible. He himself had sworn eternal enmity—and somehow never got around to it until recently, when he joined the local MIRC cell.

Weapons? The overlords possessed them, of course—but none clearly superior to those of Earth. Manpower? Clearly insufficient; there were no more than two million Kazos on all of Earth, compared to more than two billion natives. And the original ratio had been far more extended, before the almost genocidal purge of excess human population.

Even the best of administrations could not reasonably be expected to dissolve all resistance to foreign domination. Not when the subject was man. Selfish ambitions would not allow it. The average man did not want justice; he wanted all he could get, and was happy to fight for what he knew could never rightfully be his. The rich man grasped for his second fortune—not that wealth existed anymore—heedless of those who starved. The affluent nation extracted indemnities from the impoverished one. The Kazos were *fair;* that was why they should have been overthrown long ago. Man was a selfish, violent creature by nature.

Violent . . . until fifteen years ago. Then, suddenly, servile. Henrys could think of only one thing to account for the change: saturation sedation. A pacifying drug that undermined the human will to resist and conditioned the mind to accept the status quo—even when this entailed the careless tolerance of the elimination of two-thirds of the world's population within a decade. The drug could have been fed into the atmosphere, and the dosage increased whenever the situation threatened to get out of hand.

Medicinal components could contribute to general health, for that *had* improved, reducing the need for hospitalization. This was fortunate; for a time at the beginning hospitalization for even a minor complaint was tantamount to a plea for euthanasia. And gaseous fertility inhibitants would account for the general decline in births despite the mildness of penalty for violation of the one-baby rule: assignment of the surplus infants to Kazo nurseries, permanently. Those nurseries were not evil; Henrys himself had spent a decade in one. So there was now stabilization at what the overlords considered an appropriate level, and few people were eliminated anymore. Thus —peace.

Bitool led the way into a private building. Henrys was familiar with the general design of this one, as he was with every important structure in the city, but he had never entered the higher stories. It was an office skyscraper with a tremendous bookstore ensconced in the street level, a drive-in grocery chain in the basement, and, appropriately, a hydroponic division in the nether extension that fed on the adjacent sewage disposal plant. This was one of the complexes constructed under Kazo direction, replete with common sense but not always with pleasantly novel innovations.

They ignored the partial loops and took a high-velocity lift to the twentieth floor. This was actually a cross between the old-time elevators and escalators: wide, shallow compartments suspended vertically, each sufficient for two rows of five people. A man could, if he chose, ride the lift all the way to the top like a ferris wheel, then down the other side and under and back to his starting point. Henrys knew that the compartments were expressing passengers on every level of the building, above and below; the conveyance was continuous and nowhere did the shaft stand empty. Only those willing to travel in multiples of twenty stories, for the sake of speed, occupied this particular one.

The Kazos believed in efficiency.

At twenty, the lift paused for exactly two seconds. The protective outside bars shot up as the center separation fell into place. Henrys and Bitool jumped nimbly off, while other passengers jumped quickly on from the opposite side. The separation was necessary to prevent disastrous collisions between those embarking and disembarking. Henrys thought privately that this particular Kazo brainstorm was a bit too neat; a man could get killled in it!

They moved across to the slow lift that trundled along at less than a foot per second and preserved momentum by never halting at all. They waited for an empty compartment and stepped into it as it rose. At the twenty-third floor they stepped off again on the opposite side and took the conveyor down the long hall at seven feet per second.

Bitool indicated the office that was their destination and they got off. Henrys still had no idea what the overlord had in mind, or how it could relate to this routine office space. Surely the ruler of fifty million human beings was not about to waste his urgent moments assigning a strange human revolutionary to a clerical task? What could be more pressing than the problem of Kazo counteraction to the breaking storm?

For a moment Henrys wondered whether he was due for an illicit interrogation. No—no Kazo had even broken his word to an Earthman, as far as anyone could tell. The overlords simply said what they would do, and did it, without regard to the opinions of their subjects. As a man might inform his dog he was going out: what purpose, lying? That was one of the things that made them so difficult to fight: there were few valid, tangible issues. Even the mass-euthanasia program of the early years seemed to be paying off in a better life for the survivors, so that the horror of it was increasingly convenient to put aside as a necessary evil.

The interior looked more like an apartment than an office. The rooms were tastefully furnished with rugs, easy chairs, and even pictures on the wall: all Earthly. Near the far side of the main room stood a Kazo, smaller than Bitool and with lighter-hued skin. The other seemed to be uncertain—an unusual attitude among the conquerors!

Now there was a subtle change about Bitool that Henrys did not immediately understand. Could the stranger be of a higher rank? Then why the apparent reticence? There were not many that out-ranked Bitool, for he had risen steadily in the Kazo hierarchy over the years. The government on planet Kazo no doubt kept a wary eye on the administration of planet Earth, promoting those who best served the designs of the fatherworld. Bitool was capable, certainly!

"Seren." Bitool's voice interrupted Henrys' train of thought. The other Kazo turned and approached them, moving with a certain alien grace. A foreign dignitary, certainly.

Bitool took the stranger's hand and brought it to meet Henrys' own. Henrys was embarrassed for his prior thoughts about physical contact; the fingers were sinuous but warm, their pressure firm but polite.

"Richard, this is Serena, arrived this morning from Kazo." Bitool smiled carefully, human-style, and the other imitated the expression, evidently still learning. "This— she—is a, let me say, a female of our species. One of the first on Earth. You will—guide her. For three days. And return her to me."

A female Kazo, after fifteen years! No wonder Bitool was stuttering. So the species *was* bisexual, not unisexual —and now, having pacified Earth and made it safe for their kind, they meant to colonize it.

Bitool had turned abruptly and left the apartment while Henrys still held the female's hand. "Wait!" Henrys called, but he was on his own.

Serena gently disengaged her appendage. "Will you show me your planet now?" she inquired, her speech unaccented but unsure. Probably she had learned it in just the last few hours, utilizing the Kazo linguistic gift. "I know so little about it, yet."

Henrys searched for sarcasm, but detected none. It was an honest request, as it had to be, coming from a Kazo. Yet this was hardly the time! Hadn't she been told the situation in this sector?

Why had he been armed and left with her? Bitool had never bothered to obtain his formal agreement.

Someone was playing with fire. This whole affair was quite unlike the normal methodology of the conquerors. To capture the advance assassin of a human uprising and put him in charge of the first Extraterrestrial female on the planet . . .

"What did Bitool tell you about me?" he asked her.

She approached again, moving so smoothly it resembled

a glide. Her features were delicate, but she was bald and her figure could never be mistaken for that of a real girl. "Only that there would be a trusted person to guide me about the planet—"

"Trusted person!" he exclaimed involuntarily.

"And that I should follow his—your instructions dutifully. Even if they seemed strange at first." She paused. "I was alarmed—until I saw that it was you. Now I understand."

"We have never met before!"

She made a careful human shrug. "Not physically, Richard."

He digested this. For some reason she felt some affinity to him. It was an obscure female thing that Bitool had recognized and exploited. On how many devious levels did the Kazo mind operate? "Did he mention the political situation here?"

"No, Richard."

In half an hour there would be chaos in the city as the shock troops of the underground came into the open and captured the key functions of the government. If Bitool hadn't suspected the attack before, he had surely caught on when an armed Earthman came after him! Yet he had ignored the danger and turned a priceless asset over to the enemy. A Kazo female as hostage—

But Henrys had agreed, by implication, to serve the overlord for three days. He had been given no specific instructions, which meant that he had to use his own judgment. And his own ethics. That meant, in turn, that he would have to protect Serena from the violence coming, and release her in three days in some safe area if unable to return her to Bitool. It would not be honest to do less.

Bitool, of course, might be dead by then—but the obligation remained. Of all the men in the area, Henrys was probably the best equipped to preserve the life of an innocent stranger. He had been trained in espionage and knew every byway of one complex level of the city. He also knew something of the revolution's battle plan, and the key figures in it.

Bitool's action was making increasing sense. The over-lord had known that interrogation or coercion would be useless. He had also known that Henrys considered himself an honest man who did not allow the ends to justify the means. That was why he had been unable to kill the Kazo, once trust had been extended. He could have shot a cursing, ravening ET—but not a sober, intellectual individual. Bitool had wanted to put the female into safe care during the crisis, and had been guided by logic and meticulous study of his man, rather than emotion.

This new revelation of Kazo insight into human motives was chilling. Henrys had told no one of his mission. Bitool must have deduced the likely qualities for his own assassin and fed the information into the computer registry. He had known who was coming and how to deal with him—known it before Henrys himself had learned his assignment. Probably the other leading Kazos had been similarly alert. So though Henrys had never before had direct dealing with this particular overlord, their meeting was no surprise to the Kazo.

Set a thief to catch a thief—and an assassin to save a life.

"Is something wrong?" Serena asked him.

He was committed. He *had* been maneuvered into a situation he would never have chosen. Bitool had not demanded that he interfere with the revolution or give away any information concerning it—but Henrys could not protect his charge by ignoring what he knew. It was going to be difficult.

He spoke rapidly. "Serena, something *is* wrong. You will have to trust me and obey my directives implicitly, or we may both die within the hour. Do you understand?" He had never imagined he would talk this way to an overlord!

"The situation, no," she said with that typical alien candor. "But I will obey." Her ready acceptance surprised him also, for the Kazos came to Earth to give commands, not to receive them. Or was this just another aspect of the racial realism, accepting things the way they were, *what-*

ever way they were, then acting within that framework, decisively?

"There will be . . . trouble. You have perhaps twenty-five minutes to learn to pass for a human female. I'll explain once we get away from here."

"A *human?* I could not!"

Not complete acceptance, after all! He yanked open the closet door, searching for clothing. "You can't afford pride right now," he said over his shoulder. "Or modesty. I don't care how it is on Kazo, there's an emergency here. Strip down and dress as I tell you."

"Pride!" she murmured; but she began removing the smock that was evidently the Kazo traveling uniform.

Henrys found a dress and tossed it at her. "Put it on. We'll find you a long-sleeved blouse, and support stockings if we're lucky. You know what they are?"

"No, Richard."

He delved into a chest of drawers, praying that Bitool had anticipated this need, too. He had, there was a considerable assortment of lingerie, together with women's shoes, hats, and gloves. He made a selection and turned to face Serena.

She was standing in the middle of the room, the dress hanging awkwardly. She was nowhere near human in appearance. Henrys groaned and looked at his watch. Fifteen minutes—perhaps.

"I'll have to dress you myself," he said. "Close your eyes and pretend I'm a doctor, if you have to, but snap to it. It *is* a matter of life and death." How had he got into this? "Raise your arms."

She raised her arms. "I do not understand, Richard. What it it, to pretend?"

He ignored her confusion and lifted away the dress. "Brother! You're not even mammalian." But what had he expected?

"I'm sorry." Her eyes were closed.

"We'll have to fake it." He lunged at the drawer and grabbed a handful of cloth. "Take this and wad it up into balls," he said, putting the material—some kind of ker-chief—into her hands. "Open your eyes! Hurry!"

"Yes, Richard," she said, obeying.

He looped a brassiere around her chest and hooked it together on the tightest setting. She had neither ribs nor vertebrae. "Now jam that stuff into each cup, so it stands out. Sit down." He sifted through his collection and came up with panties and stockings. "Do you know how to put these on?" Ten minutes.

Neither of them knew how to keep up the heavy stock-ings; it was finally accomplished by pinning them crudely to the slip. Henrys located a feminine wig and fitted it over her head. One of her ears fell off.

He handed it to her, beyond surprise in his exaspera-tion. "Can you glue this back? Make sure your nose is on tight, too. Maybe the wig'll cover the ear . . . hold still now."

He smeared white facial cream over her head and neck. "Make sure every inch of your skin is covered by clothing or makeup," he said. "And keep that wig straight. Find two shoes that fit you, and practice walking like a lady." Her feet were three-toed and tended to splay out like those of a large bird, but he knew human shoes could be worn because Bitool had them.

She rehearsed while he gave final instructions. "You'll pose as my wife. Hang on to my arm and—"

"Pose?" she inquired. "I do not comprehend this, Richard."

Damn the forthright Kazo manner! He had five minutes to explain human ethics, or lack of them, to a person who had been born to another manner. Pretense did not seem to be a concept in the alien repertoire. How had Kazo ever overcome the earth spacefleet at the outset? The aliens *had* to have cheated—yet nothing in their makeup sug-gested that ability!

He chose another approach. "For the time being, then, you *are* my wife. Call it a marriage of convenience. A hell of a marriage and a hell of a convenience!"

She began to speak, but he cut her off. "My companion,

my female. On Earth we pair off two by two. This means you must defer to my wishes, express and implied, and avoid bringing shame upon me. Only in this manner are you permitted to accompany me in public places. Is *that* clear?"

"I am surprised your people lack the concept of female suffrage. Do you really believe that—"

"This is an emergency!" he shouted.

She fell back as if slapped. "I must conform to your local conventions," she said carefully.

"Exactly." Was he overstating the case, trying to get back at Bitool and all the Kazos by browbeating this female? Or did he resent all females, of either species? Women were *not* subject to the whims of men! "And my conventions require that you place your hand on my arm, like this—no, keep those gloves on! And stuff some paper in the extra fingers, or something!" They scrambled over the gloves, trying to make them look right. "Wait for my initiative. Nod agreement to anything I say, but moderately. Do not even think of yourself as a Kazo, for that is distasteful to me."

"But, Richard, I *am* a—"

"Of course, and we are not forgetting that for a moment. But Earth protocol requires that you minimize your origin. You don't want to insult your hosts, do you?"

"No, Richard."

"Good. As I said, I'll explain in more detail after we—"

The door burst open. A man with a machine gun entered.

Exactly on schedule—but Henrys was jogged by an incongruity. It should have taken at least half an hour for the crew assigned to this building to cover it all, even at optimum efficiency. Each man would have to check several floors. Even if this were the first floor checked in this section—how had the man reached this distant room *at the precise moment* of the inauguration of hostilities?

And why did he have a projectile weapon, when it was supposed to be a gas gun, harmless to humans but toxic to Kazos? Henrys himself had carried a projectile weapon—

but that was a special advance strike in which other humans weren't endangered. And he might have had to turn the weapon on himself.

"What is the meaning of this?" Henrys demanded, advancing upon the intruder.

The man did not recognize him. "It's the revolution, mister. We're flushing out Kazos. Stand aside while I—"

He fell, choking, as Henrys' forearm caught him across the throat. He hated to do it to one of his own people, but explanations would be suicidal—and something was fishy.

CHAPTER

5

"Here, Serena," he snapped, catching the gun and clubbing the man into unconsciousness, carefully. "Keep quiet and don't run or look around. If you have to scream, try to scream like an Earthgirl."

She was staring at the prone man. "You struck him—"

"Yeah. I'm a violent type." He took her arm and drew her to the door. "Is there anything you have to take with you? We won't be back soon."

"No, Richard," she said.

They rode the conveyor across to the express lift down. It was the same loop he had risen on, but the descending side was at the other face of the building, leading to the massed exits on the lower floors. So many people passed through this structure in any given hour that all the main passages were mechanized one-way.

Several hall doors were open, and small groups of people whispered together. Obviously the search had been proceeding all the time he was preparing Serena. It must have begun just about the time he and Bitool had entered, and the timing at the apartment was pure coincidence. Bitool had been right to leave hurriedly!

The express paused at the third floor and they jumped off. The interval remained twenty stories regardless of the floor a person started from. Each lift had a compartment for every floor, all moving as a unit. Thus the only crowding occurred on the lower floors, where everyone landed at one time or another. Henrys and Serena took the slow lift the rest of the way down.

Now he remembered to reassure her about his violence above. "I couldn't take a chance on that man recognizing you," he said under his breath. "But outside, you'll have to pass. In a crowd it'll be easier. If someone stares, ignore him."

"I do not think I look very much like a human female," she said.

"Not an attractive one," he admitted. "But the confusion connected with this revolution should help." At least, so he hoped. His precise information had been wrong on two counts—timing and weapons—so far; what other surprises awaited him?

Another man with a gun stood guard outside the building. The pedestrians ignored him much as they had Bitool; revolutions seemed to be of little interest to the populace.

Henrys averted his face to avoid being recognized and set a brisk pace down the street. "If we make it to the subway entrance, we have a good chance," he said. He had not descended to it within the building because of the likelihood of challenge by another guard. The open street was the last place to expect a walking Kazo right now, which was why it was the best place for Serena to be. "They're going after the governmental personnel and utilities first. Control those, and you control the rest! I can't risk the escape route set up for me, though—too many familiar contacts. We—"

"Richard," she said, holding back.

"Come *on!* This is no sightseeing tour."

"Richard—the pins are coming loose. The stockings—"

Despairing, he understood. The opaque stockings did not fit her Kazo-proportioned legs properly, and would fall down in a few steps without the pins. Blue legs on the city street . . .

"Grab them with your hands!" But he knew as he said

it that such a display would attract fatal attention. "No. Put your feet together and stand still. I'll get a taxi."

He could see the wrinkles forming in the loosening hose. The milling people were beginning to look. Revolutions they ignored; *this* they chose to notice! He leaped for the nearest vacant eletrotaxi parked at the corner and dumped a handful of change into its payment hopper. The door slid open across the front as the mechanism sorted and totaled the coins and hummed into life.

Henrys jumped inside and sent the car rolling forward. He halted it opposite Serena. "In!" he cried.

She hopped to the curb and twisted into the seat beside him, her movements deprived of grace. A bystander guffawed. Henrys glared at him as he slammed the wide door. He moved into traffic. "This means trouble. We have road blocks at—"

"We?"

"The revolutionists. I thought you understood that?"

"You are one of them?" she asked, perplexed. "Then why—?"

"It's a long story. Just accept the fact that I'm trying to help you. I'll do everything I can to achieve freedom for Earth, but I have to keep you out of the hands of the revolutionists."

"Yes, Richard."

"We'll have to park somewhere until the initial rush is over. We can't get out of the city until dark." He turned down a side street, alert for possible pursuit. "Get those stockings pinned again. We may be searched."

"Yes, Richard," she said, bending to the task. "I did not mean to violate protocol."

The car's dash gave a warning buzz. "Oh-oh! Two minutes to find a space," he muttered. "I don't have enough change to keep driving indefinitely."

He maneuvered into a marked spot. A red flag popped up on the meter as the vehicle's weight settled. "Damn! An hour limit. Too short," he said. He got out and drew a dollar from his wallet. "Cheaper to leave the car—but then we'd be on the street again. Got to stay."

"Will you explain?" Serena asked, joining him before the meter.

"Here on Earth you always pay too much for too little," he said. "This is one of the old dollar meters. You put the bill on the plate, like this, and you pull the handle. An alarm sounds in the police depot if the bill is counterfeit, or if you park more than two minutes on 'violation.' The meter will not accept another bill until the spot has been vacated. That's to prevent all-day parking. Doesn't really apply today, since hardly anybody bothers to drive his own vehicle—but this is the archaic level." He paused, looking at it. "Meter like this—a piece of my past."

He pulled the handle. Flag and money dropped out of sight. The needle sprang up to indicate one hour. A loud ticking commenced. "Damn inflation," he grumbled. "You used to get a full hundred minutes for the bill."

"Inflation?"

"That's when things cost more and more, making the money worth less. Actually, that stopped when the Kazos came. But this meter is fixed at the level it was at the time of conquest. Lucky, at that; at the prior rate of deterioration, that dollar would've bought only thirty minutes or less by this time."

"But can't you move to a new space after the hour, and park again?"

"I'll have to. But it increases the risk of discovery, and I only have so many dollars. We don't use them much anymore. It's best not to be too active while things are going on." He returned to the car. "Well, we have an hour. Take your seat. It's the wrong time of day, but we'll have to rely on the old lovers'-lane dodge. Do you know what I mean?"

"No, Richard."

He shrugged. "I suppose it's different on the conqueror's planet."

She turned her head to him so quickly that the wig skewed. "The *conquer* . . . oh. You are referring to planet Kazo."

"What euphemism do you prefer?" He was angry, and

knew he was taking it out on her again. "Earth was expanding into space, ready to tackle the universe, great new horizons, until—until Kazo. When I was eight years old I dreamed of becoming a hunter on a frontier planet. Every month some new world was being discovered, and some were habitable. Our aspirations were limitless. Then—"

"Yes!" she said with surprising vehemence.

"What do you know about it? How can you begin to grasp the meaning of freedom, when you have never been denied it? Have you ever been dragged screaming from a parking meter like this? Have you ever lost those closest to you? Or had to squirm under the heel of—"

"They are coming, Richard," she said, peering down the street. "Must I be silent again?"

His head snapped about. Three men with machine guns were trotting down the sidewalk. He did not recognize them, which was strange because he had thought he knew most of the members of this division. But by the same token, most of them knew *him*. "I'd better conceal my face. If any of them spot me, I'll be forced to choose between their lives and ours."

"Yes, Richard."

"I'll have to kiss you. I don't like it any better than you do."

She faced him on the seat and he twisted his shoulders and neck to meet her while shielding himself from the view of the outsiders. With a shock he realized that her lips were blue; they'd forgotten to apply lipstick!

Her face was hot, reminding him that Kazo body temperature ran about three degrees above the human norm. The makeup was already beginning to smear. He held the position while the tread of boots passed their car, paused, and went on after a lewdly suggestive whistle.

At last he felt it safe to pull away. His face was now as hot as hers. "You kiss like a woman," he said.

"Thank you, Richard." She remained as he left her, eyes closed.

"What do you do?" he asked deliberately. "Lay eggs?"

She did not react to the impertinence of the question.

"No, Richard. We give live birth, very much as men do."

"As *women* do. But no breasts?"

"The mammary glands? No, we provide predigested food for our young from our adult tract. Like, I think, your bee honey. In other respects we are very similar to you. We have families—"

"Except that you are the masters, we the slaves."

She frowned. "You do not understand, Richard. It is not that way."

"Oh? What are we humans revolting against right now, then? Our imagination?"

"I do not think you are ready to hear it, Richard."

Henrys leaned his head against the steering bar. "I was nine years old when the conqueror came," he said quietly, tired of baiting her. "We hardly knew the Kazos existed—until a year after first contact when the news came back that our fleet was lost, that our leaders had surrendered Earth itself to the alien. That evening the overlords descended upon our cities, their ships no larger, no faster than ours . . . but somehow they had vanquished us. My father was a space officer—gone, just like that. The silent spacecraft settled like the foot of a monstrous tarantula to consume our world."

"Yes," she said.

"The color of mastery was Kazo-blue. Fifteen years of it, no end in sight! The shock drove my grandmother mad; they let her live for a time, to take care of me, before classifying her surplus. I don't know why *I* wasn't fed into the euthanasia tank with the rest. I—"

"You had no mother?" she asked with a strange intensity. "You were an orphan?"

"I had a mother. My grandmother never spoke of her, but I got it from the neighborhood kids. Adultery. Her own mother—my grandmother—was outraged. Grandma had argued against the marriage, not liking association with a spaceman, but once it was done she held it sacred. Kicked her own daughter out of the house and took over. When Dad came home, when I was two, he let it stand, even though he never got along with the old lady. Dad and

Grandma and Jon—he was my friend—they were all I had, and the Conquest killed them all, really."

"Jon too?"

"He ended up in the same orphanage with me after his folks were classified surplus. Years later I saw on his record that Bitool had interceded for him; I don't know why. Then three years ago he disappeared—and I think Bitool authorized that, too. Maybe he was mixed up with the revolutionists, the same as I am now. That's *why* I mixed in—because I saw that there could be no compromise with an enemy that would wipe out a man as smart and good as Jonathan Teller."

Serena jumped, but did not comment.

"So you blanch at such murders too!" Henrys said with bitter satisfaction. "Yet you claim I don't understand."

"But it was for the benefit of the planets!" she said distractedly. "Hasn't it been a fair administration?"

He looked at her, startled by her responding intensity. "You wiped out our fleet, so that not a single man ever returned, not even for burial, when you could have spared *some*. My father was a better man than—" But that was futile. "You made our world a Kazo province, and brainwashed our people into accepting the elimination of two humans in every three—for the sake of a 'fair administration'?"

"I know your feeling, Richard! But—"

"You know my feeling," he said with flat irony. "I had to start school over to learn phonetic spelling. I grew up knowing I had only one chance in ten to be granted driving privileges. That I might marry, but never succeed in fathering more than one child of my own—and that one would be made surplus if the conqueror decided it was even marginally 'unfit.' That I could go to space only as the willing hireling of the masters. That every decision I might make was subject to alien scrutiny and approval."

"But didn't your wars stop?" she asked him eagerly. "Your disease, malnutrition, employment inequities, waste of resources—"

"Yes—by the largesse of tyranny and atmospheric in-

hibition! But better all of that, than to lose our freedom!"
He meant it, he believed it—yet once more the words remained in his memory like lines from a patriotic play.
The truth was that had the Kazoos not come, Earth might
well have exercised its vaunted freedoms—to destroy itself. His certainties were fading in the face of this Kazo
audience. "I know there were evils, but at least *we* controlled our destiny, for good *or* evil. Your rule *has* been
good, or at least necessary—better than ours, I admit—
but tyranny can't be justified merely because it is efficient."

"No, not better than yours," she murmured. "I see that
now."

"What?"

She drew back, embarrassed. She seemed momentarily
more like a girl of Earth, both in her reactions and, oddly,
her appearance. "This . . . pose . . . I am not used to
it," she said awkwardly. "But tell me, Richard—you agree
there were terrible problems before . . . us. If you were
in power, what would you do to safeguard good government?"

He frowned. Now the fugitives were talking politics, as
if it mattered! "I'm not expert on the subject, but I have
had some thoughts." He was talking to her as if she were
an equal, instead of a female overlord, yet it seemed
natural. "Our system has been like that parking meter,
there. You put your assets in and you get a measured
privilege out, whether a man or a Kazo controls the
machine. The whole world is run by a simple, unbending
standard: one dollar, one hour. One job, one wage. One
crime, one penalty, no matter what. I just don't believe
this is enough. It is bound to foul up sooner or later, because it is a mechanical standard, not a human one. People
want what they want, and they don't really care what is
proper. They look diligently for ways to get around the
standards, to jimmy the meter, beat the system, and invariably they find them."

"Is that the reason for your revolution, Richard?"

Henrys paused, taken aback. "I suppose it is."

"But is there a better system than ours—the Kazo-imposed standard?"

"There must be. I've tried to work it out, but I have only the theory, not the application. Jon was better at the practical side than I am. But I'm thinking of a piece of cake."

"A piece of cake!"

"A section from a pastry confection. Maybe you don't have cake on Kazo."

"We don't—but I have heard the expression. I understood it related to the simplicity of a dangerous mission—"

Henrys shook his head. "I never heard of that! I'm talking about edible cake—though maybe there is an analogy your way, too."

"Not *my* way. Conqueror Hen—" She stopped. "I'm sorry, Richard. I really do not know its origin! I did not mean to interrupt."

Henrys nodded, relaxing. No one else had cared to listen to his theories since Jon disappeared. "Take two children. The most important thing in the world to them, this instant, is a big piece of cake. It has to be shared between them—but their rivalry is so strong that no matter how it is sliced there will be protests and dispute. Each one demands the biggest section."

Serena put her hand on his arm, and he did not flinch. "Yes," she said, seeming to be really interested.

"An adult could make a fair division and enforce it, leaving both children disgruntled but quiet. But that's meter-justice. What happens when they are alone? The ideal system should work as well in the absence of third-party supervision."

"Go on, Richard," she said, genuinely excited.

"There *is* a system. One child gets to cut the cake; the other takes first choice. Neither one has any intention of being 'fair'—but neither can complain about the result. It works *because* of human nature, not in spite of it. I'm sure it would work with Kazos or any other species too. Now the ideal form of government—"

"Look," she said suddenly, pointing to the meter. "Our time is almost gone, and we shall have to go."

Henrys reverted to immediacies. "It's been much quieter than I expected. There can't have been much resistance." He deposited the last of his change in the car's hopper and backed out when the motor started. "It may be safe to check into a hotel now, after all."

"Will they be watching there, Richard?"

"Not if they think they've captured or killed all the overlords. They'll be too busy setting up a provisional government to bother with such details as hotel accommodations." He noted his own use of the third person with a certain detachment; there was no use denying that the steam had gone out of his revolutionary fervor.

"I hope there has not been any killing," she said.

"It wasn't their—*our* plan to kill the Kazos," he told her, omitting the chief exception. Bitool had been considered too dangerous . . . and Henrys could see why, now. "If they were willing to surrender without a fight, they'd simply be locked up. We don't want to go back to the days of murder and anarchy." But the immense supply of machine guns made him doubt the sincerity of the revolution's mysterious leader. He had not been told about those weapons, and had never met John Tanner. Certainly he had not known that the man had published a book of his principles. Yet Bitool's copy jogged inside his shirt, showing that the overlord had known more about the rebel leader than Henrys did.

Had mass executions been arranged? Serena might be the only living Kazo in this sector! "But you'll have to stay with me until we are sure," Henrys said.

"I understand, Richard."

He hoped she did *not!* He parked the car at one of the recharging stands and showed the way to a hotel. At the door he stopped her. "Do you have any lipstick?"

"Lipstick, Richard?"

"Never mind. I'll bluff it, if the clerk notices. But stay behind me and out of the light, if you can." He had chosen this hotel because it was old-fashioned, even for this level, with human help. That should reduce the risk. A mechanized house would automatically register their human identities with the general computer—and of course Serena had none. Not human. The revolutionists would have control over the computer files by this time—with one Richard Henrys listed as a traitor. No—more likely they thought him dead. That was better. Later, he could explain it all to somebody. Not now.

"Yes?" a voice said in that special tone.

Oh no, he thought. *Not one of the sanctimonious ones!* Fortunately he didn't know the man. "Room for two."

The clerk peered at him over rimless spectacles: an affectation, since the poor-of-sight had long since been made surplus. "You have a reservation?"

"No."

"We shall have to verify your credit rating."

"Cash." Fortunately, again, he retained some larger bills. But how long would his luck hold out?

"Very good, sir," the clerk said, his tone conveying eloquently what he thought of barbarians who stooped to cash. Henrys almost laughed; this character really put his soul into his part!

The man made out the registry. "Your wife looks cold, sir."

"I'm not his—" Serena began, forgetting.

"Appearances can be deceiving," Henrys said, interrupting her.

The clerk did not laugh. "Her lips—"

"She's recovering from an illness." Now he was lying. Where was that integrity he had prided in himself? Did it vanish upon the first inconvenience? Yet what else could he do?

"We have a doctor—"

Would tthe man never give up? "No thanks. Rest cure. Nothing contagious. An evening's relaxation will work wonders. You know how it is."

The clerk frowned. "I see. The room charge includes a tranquilizer."

Expensive tranquilizer! Henrys decided, however, not

to protest the size of the bill, though it almost wiped him out. How would he manage the remaining two days, after depleting his resources in one? But again he seemed to have no choice.

The tranquilizer was waiting as they entered the room: about eighty-six proof and quality vintage. Henrys reddened as he comprehended the clerk's assessment of his motives. No doubt places like this were popular for liaisons.

Serena picked up the bottle, intrigued. She did not seem to be nearly as concerned for her safety as Henrys was. Perhaps that was just as well.

"It's a beverage," Henrys explained. "Intended for human consumption. In extreme moderation. I'd advise caution."

"Oh, a Kazo can digest anything you can," she assured him brightly. "I cooked for—" She negotiated the seal by wrapping one sinuous finger around it and pulling, surprising Henrys with her leverage. She found a tumbler and poured herself about four ounces. Did she always have so many unfinished thoughts? For whom had she cooked, back on Kazo? And what was the relevance?

Henrys watched with dismay as she lifted the whiskey to her blue lips and downed it neat. "An *alcoholic* beverage," he said. "It depresses the higher centers of control and leads eventually to a comatose state. I wouldn't—"

"No effect on Kazo metabolism," she said, pouring herself another liberal dose. "I like it."

Henrys let the matter go, hoping she was right. "I promised to explain why this subterfuge was necessary. I didn't mean to place you in a compromising situation, but—"

"Compromising, Richard?"

He checked the fixtures for spying devices, just in case, though he was sure the revolutionists would not have such things organized yet. "Ordinarily a man and a woman do not share a room unless they are married."

"But you explained about that, Richard."

She still didn't seem to grasp the principles of expediency or euphemism. "Of course we are of totally different species—"

"No objections," she said easily. "Do you know, Richard, this bev-beverage is very good. Are you sure you won't have some before I finish it?"

"*Finish* it!" Henrys was aghast—but saw that the level actually was low. A full fifth almost gone! "Are you *sure* it doesn't affect you? We have to keep alert."

"Richard, our entire met-meta—our entire chemistry is different, however similar our minds may be. We can consume the same foods, but once they enter the system . . . for example, that man was wrong about my being cold. The present temperature is entirely comfort . . . nice for me." She plopped into the easy chair, letting her wig fall askew.

Henrys suddenly remembered the lipstick and began checking the room's appointments. If they were lucky—

"You're not mammals," he said irritably. "You don't shiver or sweat. How *do* you control your body temperature?" He already had some notion, as the information was available in the libraries, but he had decided it was better to keep her talking. Otherwise her natural curiosity could get them into further trouble.

Serena fished a magazine out of the wastebasket beside her chair. Evidently cleanup was perfunctory here, despite the price of admission. She turned the pages as she spoke. "We possess an internal quantity of heat-retentive fluid that acts as a reservoir. Not blood—similar perhaps to your lymph system—no, not that either. Anyway, this accumulates surplus calories in the daytime exercise and dispenses it at night, stabilizing the . . . There is also a certain amount of avoir-avoirdupois around the body that can be redistributed as protection against localized exposure."

"And to mimic the shape of other species, I understand," Henrys muttered. It was said that a Kazo could make himself up to look exactly like a man, if he wanted to; but he had never actually seen that, and assumed it was an exaggeration. With all the trouble he had had passing

Serena off . . . ! Taking his cue from her, he sorted through the bathroom trash basket. There, wonderfully, he found it: the remnant of a tube of lipstick. It was not usable as it stood, but there was still substance in the base. He pried at it with a penknife. "Suppose you have a heat-wave?"

"A caloric overload? No problem," she said, her voice slurring slightly. He tried to convince himself it was because she was attemping to read the magazine while talking, but the picture in his mind was of the empty whiskey bottle. That much alcohol, in that time, could be fatal to a human being—or at least make him extremely sick. And drunk.

"On the surface of our limbs," she continued, eyes still on the text, "are fine metallic fibers that radiate excess energy efficiently when required. I believe the principle is similar to what you employ for mechanical refrigeration. You convey the heat to a radiating—"

Henrys, having pried open the tube, looked at her directly. He saw the cover of the issue she was reading: a girlie magazine. He hoped she didn't understand it.

"Let's get some of this on your lips," he said. "We can't have them showing blue."

"All right, Richard," she agreed. "You had better apply it, however. You know what you want."

He knelt beside her and touched the blob of red to her mouth. "It isn't what *I* want," he said. "It's to conceal your identity until you can rejoin your own kind. No Kazo is safe in this city, at the moment."

"This is an interesting publication," she said as he finished a somewhat blotchy job. "But I'm not clear on certain things. Why are—"

"It's part of the props for this level," he explained. "Everything has been maintained as it was, even the trashy magazines. For verisimilitude."

"Yes. Why are there no pictures of human males presented here? It says it is for men, and they are quite active in the descriptions. In fact, I had not realized humans were capable of repeated—"

"Never mind!"

"And are the female proportions accurately represented? I did not see many young women on the street, but they were not—"

"The women depicted," Henrys said without emphasis, "are not typical. They represent the supposed ideal as determined by the criteria of frustrated masculine editors. Today this is hardly relevant, because of social reforms the overlords imposed, and such material becomes humorous. But then—"

"But this concentration on the physical—"

"A man pays attention to the physical attributes, particularly those of face and torso. That's why I put a wig on you and had you stuff your, uh—so that nothing would be out of place."

"My 'uh . . .' " she murmured, looking down her front. "But why should it matter, Richard? I realize I had to be concealed—but why should it be so important even in a naturally human female?"

Didn't they have sex-appeal on planet Kazo? "These visible characteristics may determine the extent of a man's immediate interest in a given specimen. If a woman *looks* capable of effective reproduction—"

Serena found a few more drops in the bottle. "How convenient! That seems so much more forthright than our own system. Shape, rather than character! And I am to emulate a woman. Let me see. . . ." She stood up unsteadily and tugged at her dress.

"What are you doing?" Henrys asked with alarm.

"I am removing my clothing, Richard. Just as described in this publication." She swayed, but got the dress over her head.

Henrys turned away. "Oh. You will find the shower in there. The bathroom."

"Water? I do not need it, thank you, Richard."

"I think you do. A good, *cold* blast—"

But obviously she did not understand. He stood with his back to her, uncertain what to do. It was obvious that he had an intoxicated Kazo female on his hands. He did not know what to expect next, but hoped it wouldn't be messy; almost certainly it meant trouble. She was a member of a species far more divergent from his own than any native to Earth—but he had come to accept her as sapient and female, and could no longer view her with indifference.

She was moving around busily, and once the magazine rustled, as if she were rechecking a detail. "Please give me your opinion, Richard," she said at last.

He turned, assuming that she had adjusted her dress and donned it again more comfortably. He was mistaken.

She had stripped herself of all apparel except the wig, and now displayed a stunningly human outline. There were enormous breasts where her chest had been flat before, and her hips flared. The waist narrowed alarmingly.

Henrys forgot himself and stared. "What—?"

"Is everything in order, Richard? I modeled it after the illustrations—"

He studied her body, appalled. The flesh was real. She was exactly like a buxom model dipped in blue. How had she done it?

Then he remembered her explanation about avoirdupois, and the stories about Kazo mimicry. She had intended it literally when she talked about redistribution of flesh. That would also explain the Kazo similarities of facial feature; they could shape their flesh and cartilage to match the human structure, except for such small projections as nose and ears.

He had told her to pass herself off as a human female, not realizing how far she would take it.

"If the physique is satisfactory," she said, "I am ready to conform to the rest of your conventions, Richard."

He had been inspecting her as if she were a statue. She was certainly statuesque! He turned away, reddening again. "Conventions?"

"To be your wife, your companion, your female, as you directed. So that no one will suspect my Kazo identity. I did not understand it entirely, before, but there are several detailed descriptions of the procedure in the publication."

CHAPTER
6

◆ ◆ ◆

Henrys choked. She had applied the erotica to the original subterfuge, not penetrating the true nature of either. "This applies only in public," he said as evenly as he could. "There is no sexual compatibility between our species. As you surely are aware."

There was a pause. "I'm sorry, Richard. Did I make an error in the pose? Too much intoxication?"

Pose? "You mean to say you're *not* drunk?"

"Yes, Richard." The fuzziness and hesitation vanished. She *had,* it seemed, grasped some of it. The feminine artifice!

Henrys shook his head. "Serena, what—suppose I *had* meant it literally? What kind of a game did you think you were playing?"

"You seemed sincere," she said. "And you addressed me by my intimate name. You have taken great risks to yourself to keep me from harm. And you *are* the—no, I forget. That is changed."

"You keep making oblique references to something I don't know about! What do you know that—"

"On planet Kazo a female of my status is normally addressed by only part of her name. And often the males, too. I should have told you that before."

"That isn't what I meant! You know something—"

71

"You do not find me attractive?"

"I do *not*. Not that way. But what I was asking—"

"This is not what I would have said to you, Richard."

He took a deep breath. "Serena—I mean *Seren*—get dressed and I'll try to clarify things."

She dressed silently. He was upset about hurting her feelings, but realized that strict truth was the only course to follow from here on.

"Since Earth fell to the invader," he said, "we have had only one serious hope for freedom: that the occupation was temporary. That the Kazos would one day go away. We know that it is impossible to throw off the alien yoke by force; this entire revolution exists only by Kazo sufferance, and will collapse when the first genuine counteraction is taken. That isn't what the leaders think, but it is the truth."

"You said you were part of it, Richard. Don't you believe in it?"

"I—" He paused, baffled. "I thought I did. But when they sent me to—"

She glanced at him alertly, no trace of intoxication in her manner.

"To kill the overlord Bitool," Henrys continued with difficulty. "I—but I don't believe in taking life. I would never—"

She modified the subject delicately. "What were you about to say about your attitude toward Kazo females, Richard?"

He sat down. The book Bitool had given him shifted inside his shirt—how had he forgotten it so long!—and he drew it out. "I have to hate the Kazo female. Every person on Earth must feel the same. Because the occupation can be considered temporary only so long as the conqueror does not colonize. The moment he starts bringing in family units, he has given notice he means to stay. Kazo females are incompatible with the freedom of Earth."

"Yes," she said in that way of hers.

But as he spoke, his eyes were on the title, *The Revolutionist's Handbook,* and his thoughts were in a third domain. How could he ever have agreed to kill anyone, any creature? It was an act of barbarity that repulsed him utterly. Yet he had fired twice at Bitool. . . .

"I comprehend your point," Serena said. "But Bitool assigned you to take care of me. He knew, as I know—"

Then the author's name leaped up at him, making a connection whose full significance had somehow evaded him before. John Tanner. The leader of MIRC: the present revolution. Whose book was in the hands of the Kazos, but had not been shown directly to the partisans. And Bitool had urged him to read it.

It *was* ridiculous to assign a known assassin to the protection of the first female colonist. Unless there was collusion of some sort between the overlords and the revolutionary leadership. Would this book explain it all?

He opened it. There in the preface were the very sentences he had spoken in answer to the overlord's rapid queries: automatic responses, rote replies from a printed catechism he did not recall ever studying. "A revolutionist is one who desires to discard the existing . . . "

He flipped to the title page. "John Tanner, M.I.R.C. (Member of the Idle Rich Class)."

A joke. And at the foot, a brief note: "Reprinted from the supplement to the play *Man and Superman,* by George Bernard Shaw, in which John Tanner is a fictional character."

"Something is wrong, Richard?"

Henrys hurled the book from him. "I've been a patsy. They must have drugged me and instilled posthypnotic suggestion and a headful of platitudes—and Bitool knew it! He knew I was doped and duped. Probably my whole escape route was phony, and most of the information I thought I had. If I killed Bitool and got captured myself, none of my information would mean a thing!"

"Then you are not of their number?"

"I *thought* I was of their number," he said, chagrined. "All my philosophizing . . . my 'piece of cake.' I thought I was on the way to answers. I thought I had something useful to do."

"Perhaps you still do, Richard. Why did you assist me, even against the men you believed were your compatriots?"

"What a man believes may be ascertained," he said in a rapid monotone, "not from his creed, but from the assumptions on which he habitually acts." He laughed harshly. "That's another dear little quote from the handbook. I recognize it now. The irony is that much of it does make sense. It was easy for me to believe I believed it. I *do* believe it, or at least I agree with much of it. I helped you because I had given my word, or the equivalent—and you needed help. That was something quite apart from automatic phrases."

"I am very glad that was the case, Richard."

"But I *still* don't approve of the Kazo rule. Men should be allowed to make their own mistakes. It isn't fair to—" He stopped, listening.

Heavy boots were tramping down the old wooden boards of the hall.

"Out the window!" he snapped. "We're lucky this hotel is confined to the archaic level, instead of—"

She moved immediately at his direction, asking no questions. It was as though she were used to taking orders from humans. He loosed the catch and knocked the window open. His training might be little more than hypnotic indoctrination for this isolated mission, but it stood him in good stead now. He knew what had happened and what to do. The clerk had become suspicious and requested a computer check on their identities. Thus the true revolutionaries had traced him and come to recover the invaluable Kazo female, a hostage to make the revolution valid.

He was hungry. He thought of it, oddly, as he bustled Serena down the metal steps of the bottom segment of a classic fire escape and on into the evening. He had not eaten since this misadventure started, and she was probably no better off, despite the calories in the liquor.

A long, ancient, filthy alley ran beside the hotel, as ugly as such corridors had traditionally been since the days of Babylon, when the very pavement had been constructed of packed garbage. They trotted down it. He had always thought of the archaic level as a monument to the prior greatness of Earth, but now he realized that it also signified the horrors of public indifference.

His comprehensive knowledge of the city streets stood him in good stead, again. This was honest information, years in the acquisition; no one could outmaneuver him here. Just ahead there was a—

A beam of light pierced the shadow, searching for them from the window just quitted, but there was no outcry. He jerked Serena around the corner. Fitting irony: his fake indoctrination made him far more competent at this game than his pursuers were. They had thought to march in noisily and catch him napping.

The lighted entrance to the subterranean transit was at hand. They merged with the evening throng. At the first level down they stepped onto a belt traveling toward the center of town and stood together like a couple going on a date. Serena retained her body, and it strained at the more conservative dress, but she had not forgotten to straighten her wig and powder her face during the flight. She even attracted a complimentary glance or two.

Henrys had chosen this belt because it moved in the opposite direction expected of a person fleeing the city. Now it occurred to him that he was being foolish. Either the revolutionists were after him and wanted him badly enough to close off every city exit—a phenomenal undertaking, on top of the problems of the takeover—or their interest in him was incidental. He had jumped to the conclusion that they had spotted him in the hotel, but now he saw this as a conditioned response, and an exaggeration of his importance. It could have been someone on an unrelated errand—and probably no one but Bitool knew about Serena.

And he had sacrificed the room he had paid for, on that wild suspicion. Now he lacked the funds for another. His conditioning had not helped him, it had betrayed him.

"Seren," he murmured. "I think I have miscalculated.

Are you willing to take a chance? Maybe a dangerous one?"

"Yes, Richard."

He guided her off the belt at the next travelers' aid station. The man looked up as they approached the booth. "Yes?" he inquired, very much as the hotel clerk had.

"We are travelers not in sympathy with the uprising," Henrys said quickly. "We do not have money for food and credit while the rebels—"

"Take a seat, please," the clerk said without changing expression. He touched a button on his phone.

They sat down uneasily on the bench facing the booth. "Are you certain that was wise?" Serena inquired.

"No." He wondered whether her concern was for the amount of information given away, or because he had not been entirely candid with the clerk. *She* might have stated the whole truth. "It is a calculated risk. He will either find facilities for us that are discreet—or he will betray us to the revolution. If he reports us, be ready to move in a hurry; we should be able to lose ourselves again."

"Yes, Richard."

"But the odds are that no chase is on, and this way we'll have the benefit of—"

A man strode up to the counter, robust and solid, with a receding hairline and a round cheerful face. The clerk said something in a low tone, not looking up, and the man moved on. Henrys relaxed.

Then a man with a machine gun rode down the belt. Henrys tensed and touched Serena on the arm. He tried not to stare or reach for his own weapon, but no one else was paying any attention. It was amazing how sanguinely the populace took the revolution. Or was it merely the old, old policy of noninvolvement, euphemized as "live and let live" or "the golden rule"?

"The golden rule is that there are no golden rules," he murmured, quoting from Tanner again. How could a man witness an atrocity, and ignore it in the name of anything golden?

But he knew that no one would help him if the armed

man attacked. He would have to use his palm pistol or run.

The revolutionist rode on by.

"Will you join me?" It was the robust man, now seated beside them. Henrys had been so anxious about the armed man that he had not paid enough attention to his immediate surroundings.

Should he trust this person? Obviously this was the clerk's contact.

What choice did he have? "Thank you," he said.

The man stuck out a healthy hand. "Adam Notchez, master sergeant, World Army, retired."

They shook hands. "Dick Henrys—and this is Serena."

Notchez escorted them to a handsome apartment in the modern high-rise residentials. Henrys was relieved to get clear of the archaic level, though of course the revolutionists didn't care where he was. "My grandchildren are about somewhere. 'Hide and tag' in the lift, most likely."

Henrys could imagine it: ride to a random floor, jump off, jump on again after several compartments had passed, while the pursuing child had to outguess the first and catch up without overshooting. To watch the floors from a compartment, or the compartments from one floor? Endless possibilities. "Is that permitted?" he inquired.

"Of course not! I'll have to pretend I don't suspect. That's why I'm a popular baby-sitter: I'm good at keeping secrets. Kids don't have the interaction they used to, with only one to a family, so the cousins need to get together like this. Got nothing better to do with my time, these days. Have a drink?"

"No!" Henrys said, cutting Serena off. She smiled faintly and winked at Notchez, who grinned back.

"Well, you're both hungry, I know. It'll have to be leftovers, though. Hydro-turnip salad, soy milk, the usual. I sure miss the old days."

Henrys tensed. "You object to Kazo rule?"

Notchez gestured expansively as he set down the food. "Ten years ago I would have been in the forefront of the mob, howling for blue blood. Five years ago I might have supported a revolution tacitly. But now that it's come, I discover that I don't go for it. Suddenly I find myself appreciating fifteen consecutive years of peace and prosperity. That's a world record, you know. It beats the old one by about fourteen and a half years. Oh, I miss it, all that action and uncertainty. I get terribly nostalgic—but I don't regret it."

"Didn't you suffer losses in the purge?" Henrys asked.

Notchez nodded soberly. "I had six kids, and four got taken for surplus. That's when I would've killed the blues! But later—years later!—I realized that the weakest had been culled. One had a heart condition, and that's hell when it starts in youth. Another was pretty wild, went on destroy-tantrums. And two were having bad trouble in school. I just wasn't such great shakes as a father. But the two who were really strong, smart, and healthy—well, now they've got those kids of their own. And I was one of six myself—and three died before the Kazos came, and another was in a hospital, permanently, you know. So the ratio was just about the same. If four out of six have to go, better they go selectively. And cleanly. That knockout beam doesn't hurt, you know—just fades you into a sweet dream, and then nothing."

"Nothing but fertilizer," Henrys muttered.

"But weren't you in Earth's military?" Serena asked, nibbling delicately on a flavored mushroom. "Those were the first taken, weren't they?"

Henrys tightened, but the sergeant didn't seem to notice the signal of alien viewpoint: *Earth's* military.

"Thirty years!" Notchez laughed. "No, they were selective there, too. Oh, I know what you're going to say next! What does a career man do, when there isn't any war? And I shall inform you that the army is with us yet, and the navy too—busier than ever. The war never stopped. Not for an instant."

Henrys put his hand on his concealed pistol.

"The war against hunger, disease, ignorance," their host continued. "It took me a long time to be convinced. I was so sure there was an ulterior motive, that the overlords were setting us up for something terrible—extinction of the species, for example, or reduction to slavery for Kazo colonists. But I changed my mind. Here, let me show you." He touched a button and a projection came to life on the wall opposite them. Notchez hiked his chair around beside Henrys.

"This is the Global Highway. The Kazos decided that civilization depended on good communications, and that meant among other things high capacity arteries. This is the mightiest turnpike ever built on Earth—sixteen lanes across, twelve tiers tall. The Romans were pikers!"

Henrys smiled at the sergeant's little joke. Pike—pikers. He knew about the highway, though he had never driven on it. Serena was watching the projection with her usual interest.

The highway rose like the Wall of China, a hundred feet high and twice as wide, yet sunlight filtered through its several layers and green plants decorated every level. The camera panned across the continuous restaurants, recharging stations, theaters and hotels lining its center mall, all elegantly sculpted and brilliantly clean. Electric cars shot by at a hundred and fifty miles per hour in the isolated speed lanes, while they seemed to inch along at thirty in the outer scenic strips.

"My unit was never even broken up," Notchez was saying. "We were redesignated a construction battalion, and our chain of command descended from a Kazo general. He was an old line space officer, knew nothing about construction, but he was a hell of an organizer. We worked on that road—and I tell you, I learned more about building, the last dozen years of my enlistment, than I ever thought I'd know about anything. We had to excavate fifty feet into the ground and level it, come mountain or ocean, sticking mostly to contour, and pipe the rivers through along with animal-crossing conduits. The pike runs from Cape Horn to the Cape of Good Hope without a break, splitting into the Siberian/European/West African and the South Asian loops that join up again at the equator. I worked on sections in five continents and the Indonesian Spur."

There was a shot of one of the underground lanes, as seen from a speeding car. The walls on either side were decorated with murals: scenery similar to that visible along the various other sections. For a change in view, the driver could shift to another lane, relieving the monotony. An inset picture of the speedometer showed it rising above the posted limit.

"Watch this," Notchez said proudly.

At five kilometers per hour over the limit the mural wavered and dissolved into inchoate patches of color. The scene had been of mountains, and the effect was startling —as if an earthquake had developed and shaken them apart. Enough to jolt the average driver into awareness.

At ten kph over, enormous letters appeared: OVER-SPEED.

"Damnedest effect," the sergeant observed. "Something about the optics of it. The car sets up sympathetic vibration in the air, too, at that speed, making a most unpleasant keening noise. Same thing happens if you go too slow. Of course speeders *are* arrested if they push their luck— and one deliberate offense costs 'em their driving privileges forever. Now watch."

The dial of the speedometer dropped and the mural re-appeared. Henrys realized that the picture was enormously elongated, to provide a natural effect when viewed at speed—yet the distant mountains shifted perspective realistically while near objects blurred by. This was not a simple painting.

The indicator dropped below the minimum posted and the picture blurred again. No words appeared at the reduced velocity, however; instead the colors jumped, as though on separate frames.

Then he understood. They *were* separate frames—wide columns angled to present a compensated view of sections of color: red, yellow, and blue. Between these posts he could now make out the adjoining lanes, and *their* pillars, a subterranean concrete forest. The proper speed combined the sections into a full-color, continuous image, while improper velocity brought out another illustration, as though stroboscopically phased. Yet it was mechanical, not electronic; art and technology combined in a useful application of known principles.

Notchez was answering one of Serena's questions. "Well, I think the cars are supposed to be spaced a hundred feet apart, on the average, though of course traveling speed makes a difference. Say they're doing sixty—that's over fifty cars passing any given point in each lane. Ninety-six lanes going each direction—call it five thousand cars per minute, total, each way. Comes to—I figured it out once—about seven hundred thousand every twenty-four hours—east or west. Put a family of three in each car, and in three years you could empty the planet."

"And you built it all in only twelve years?" Serena inquired. The projection was riding along the top section now, the only level that *looked* like a highway. The view was from the innermost lane, overlooking the mall; the tops of trees waved at eye-level, and swinging pedestrian mock-vine ramps crossed to the other side. The pike itself was a tourist attraction.

"Thirty thousand miles of it? No—there's still a gully cooling off in the Urals and a couple other places, where they had to 'H' a channel. Can't build until the radiation stops, you know. And down in Sumatra and Java, between the monsoons and the earthquakes—"

The door slid open and two children appeared, interrupting him. Notchez turned off the image. "Kids, you know how late it is? Know what your folk would say to me if they knew—?"

One was a girl about six; the boy was a little smaller. "We won't tell if you don't, Granpa," the girl said precociously. She spied the visitors. "Oh. Hello, visitors."

"Hello," Serena answered promptly.

"Kazo!" both children screamed, rushing at her.

Henrys' hand dived for his weapon, but this time the host's heavy arm slapped him back against the chair. "You don't make that motion twice—not against an army man," Notchez murmured. His iron grip closed on Henrys' wrist. "Just keep quiet and watch."

Henrys could have put the man to sleep, regardless. But the damage was already done. He kept quiet and watched.

"Kazo!" the little girl repeated, as each child clung to one of Serena's arms and tugged at the gloves to reveal the blue skin and alien hands beneath. But they were smiling.

"You knew all the time," Henrys snapped.

"I worked under Kazo supervision a dozen years," Notchez said. "For the last five I was Enlisted Liaison man for the general. I know a Kazo when I see one, though I never saw a female before." His grip relaxed. "And I guess the kids do too. I didn't think they'd be that quick!"

The gloves dropped to the floor. "See?" the girl exclaimed triumphantly. "All blue!"

"I always told them that only good children could ever get to meet a Kazo," Notchez explained. "As I said, my attitudes changed quite a bit over the years. There's pain in the past, a lot of it—but now I respect what the overlords have accomplished, and I know this is the way it has to be, and I am far from being alone. That's why I agreed to hide you during the . . . disturbance."

"The travelers' aid man knew too?" Henrys asked, upset.

"No. This Kazo's pretty well camouflaged; flesh looks real, even. But I knew some Kazos would get caught in the open . . . ." He shrugged. "You'll stay here for the duration. The children wouldn't have it otherwise. Their folk won't be back until tomorrow, and they'll understand. Or do you doubt the kids' motives?"

The little boy climbed into Serena's lap and was whispering something into her imitation ear, while the girl yanked at him jealously. Henrys hoped her features would stay in place under this attack.

"You will find that this 'revolution' is pretty much shrugged off by the average man," Notchez continued. "There is always a ruthless lunatic fringe. But the great majority have come to realize, as I have, that the loss of the Kazos would be the greatest disaster Earth could sustain. The yoke is light, the benefits impressive. In a few days those self-styled saviors of man are going to crawl back into their holes, baffled by human contempt and passive resistance. They're out of date by a decade. We don't need their kind anymore."

"But would you feel that way without—"

"Without being drugged?" Notchez shrugged. "If the atmosphere is loaded the way the soreheads claim, would revolution ever have broken out? Seems more likely that we're free agents now, whatever we were before."

Why hadn't he thought of that? The fact of the revolution did give the lie such pacification. His thoughts and feelings had to be his own, unless the revolutionists had found some individual antidote. If they had, why hadn't they given it to everyone? Unless they *wanted* passivity so *they* could rule. Either way, the Kazos seemed to be vindicated. Henrys didn't have to resent what he suspected they had done to his emotions.

"I think I have some cake somewhere," Notchez said, standing. "If it doesn't start a riot."

"Me first!" the children cried in unison, scrambling after him.

Henrys let the burden of doubt fall away. "If you will allow me to make a suggestion—"

"But I want some too, Richard," Serena protested mischievously.

The sergeant emerged from the kitchenette with half of a richly frosted chocolate cake. "Isn't what we knew in the old days," he said, "but it tastes the same—and I guess nutrition is as good from sewage as from sugar." He set it down. "My personal drug indicator is a piece of cake," he continued, making Henrys start. "If I can divide it peacefully, I figure the suppressant is acting. Tonight I know there'll be a row!"

"Even so, it can be done," Henrys said. "Drugs aren't necessary if you allow for human nature. It's just a matter of—"

"But *everyone* should have a piece," Serena said.

"Fine," Notchez agreed. "Just so long as it's divided fairly, and *I* get the fairest chunk!"

Henrys contemplated the prize. "You conspirators think you have me licked, don't you?"

They laughed, and the children clapped their hands, aware that something interesting was developing.

"Well, try *this* for size," Henrys said. "There are five of us, er, equals. Nobody wants to be deprived, right? Very well: I will cut myself a section representing my fair share—one fifth. If any of you think it is too big for me, you may cut off a little to make it right. OK? Then you can divide the rest of the cake among you, crumbs and all, in the same fashion."

The little girl stood on one foot and screwed up her face in concentration. "I get last choice," she announced after a moment. The boy was silent, not comprehending this, suspicious of a ruse.

"Your piece may become rather small," Notchez warned Henrys.

Henrys grinned. "One small clarification: the last person to touch the piece gets it instead."

Now all were perplexed except Serena, who refrained from comment. "You are sure this thing will get off the ground?" Notchez inquired dubiously.

Henrys took the knife and cut off a full quarter. "There's my piece," he said, licking his lips. "Anybody object?"

"Yeah!" the children cried, appalled at such gluttony. They did not comprehend the mathematics of fractions, but could tell the piece was oversize. The girl snatched the knife and assessed the situation. "I can take away as much as I want?"

"Yes. But then you keep the piece left, unless someone else touches it after you."

"But what if I make it too small?"

"Too bad."

She hovered over it, unable to make up her mind. Finally she shaved off a thin segment and swept it into the main body of the cake. "There. Now it's mine."

"Oh, yeah?" her cousin demanded. He knocked off a tiny crumb. "Mine!"

She glared at him. The piece was still a generous one.

"Next?" Henrys said.

No one moved.

"Mine!" the boy exclaimed again, gleefully. He made off with the booty. The girl looked angrily after him, but did not speak.

"I begin to glimpse the light," Notchez said. He took the knife and severed a smaller piece. No one challenged it, and it was his. "Yes—I comprehend!"

Serena took another slim section, leaving the last decision between Henrys and the girl. "I'll cut—you choose. Okay?" he asked her.

She nodded warily. He divided it unevenly.

She stared. "My choice?"

"Right."

She squealed with delight. "You made a mistake!" she cried, pouncing on the larger piece

"Can't win 'em all," Henrys observed philosophically.

"But you see it would be cumbersome to divide a cake between two billion people that way," Bitool said. "That is the weakness of that system. By the time it could be accomplished, the cake would have rotted, and the people starved, even if social problems could be arbitrated so simply. The fair way is not always the best way."

Henrys looked out the window of Bitool's office, wondering where the overlord and other Kazos had concealed themselves for the past three days. Not one had been captured by the armed searchers. Serena could have hidden with them, obviously, with perfect safety—yet she had risked her life among the humans instead. Why?

The revolutionists had abdicated in the face of massive indifference, as predicted, and had accepted exile on a Pacific isle helpfully deeded to them. In the name of freedom they had made themselves prisoners. The coup itself had never even made headlines. "I know," Henrys said, "that the world cannot properly be equated to a piece of cake. Simile goes only so far. But I'll stand by this principle: there must be a way to achieve commerce between species without the conquest of one by the other. Some way to divide and choose—"

He broke off. "Just what *did* happen to the Earth fleet, at the beginning?"

"Tell him, Seren."

Serena, now of normal Kazo appearance without ears and nose, closed her eyes and spoke in a strange, impassioned singsong: "It is the year of the flightless amphibian, of the bloom of the seaborn ones, and of our fourteenth offworld colony. Our ships range into the realm of null-communication, searching out strange worlds, and we are waiting for more news of wonder. Only in space are we united, and soon even that may fall away, as we find no common enemy to bind our passions together. Yet we fear that theoretic enemy even more, for we are new to space and our hold on it is uncertain.

"And our fleet gathers its ships of all dependencies and disappears—and then the horde of the Earthman comes and we are surrendered and we do not know what has happened. We had not even known Earth existed, until it conquered! We try to resist, but our governors are gone over to the enemy and we are become hostage to our own weapons. And the human creatures emerge from their loud battleships, beings of ferocious aspect and immobile feature, of stiff limbs and many weak fingers, some pale as bone or black as earth, all of astonishing tenacity, and we are afraid.

"They kill us, whole families at a time, exterminating one in every two. But they are fair, policing their own numbers as rigidly as ours, and in time we come to know that there is glory behind their power and sorrow beneath their regimentation. We chafe under their harsh mastery, seeing them no more advanced than we—but we forget our terrors of war and famine, for peace is absolute."

"*Earth* conquered *Kazo?*" Henrys demanded numbly. "*You* suffered the loss of your friends and relatives?"

"My family was surplus," she said. "Fomina interceded

to save me, and Conqueror Henrys took me into his home in her stead—"

"Fomina!" Bitool said, stricken.

"My father!" Henrys cried almost at the same time.

"He had agreed to preserve her," Serena said. "As Bitool agreed to preserve you, Richard. But it had to be within the system, so as not to begin corruption—and she would not be saved. Conqueror Henrys grieved for her as if she were his own. I stayed with him for many years, learning of his sincerity, and though I thought I hated the Conqueror, I came to love—"

Bitool expressed the first shock Henrys had seen in a Kazo. "I did not know this, Seren!"

"You have not been on the homeworld, Bitool," she said. "Surely you guessed there was reason I came first to your sector, despite the unrest? Through me you learn what your pact accomplished. It should have been Fomina—"

"No fault of yours," Bitool said quickly. "I understood the necessity of sacrifice at the outset, and the years have mellowed my grief. It is enough to know she chose her own course."

"I knew it was wrong," she continued quietly. "But the temptation I dared not try on the father I had to try on the son, for they are similar. With no success."

Henrys was elated and embarrassed and horrified all at once as he tried to assimilate the elements of these confessions.

"This was not intended," Bitool said, not well controlled himself. "There must be no such relationships between the species."

"So Conqueror Henrys felt, also," Senera said with a certain difficulty. "Naïveté, in you both. How else is one to find common ground with the Conqueror?"

Henrys would have been amused at this example of differing attitudes of Kazo-male and Kazo-female—or perhaps of conqueror-Kazo and conquered-Kazo—if his own fate were not so intimately connected. He put aside the personal implications and fixed momentarily on the political picture. "Do you mean Earth and Kazo *exchanged governments?*"

Serena smiled "I was surprised too, Richard. Perhaps I did not fully appreciate it until you explained about the cake. But isn't it best?"

"But how can you be sure the Earthmen aren't brutalizing your home? I realize Bitool and my father made a private deal—but that's only a little part of—"

Bitool recovered his serenity. "Richard, do you expect us to send men to govern our own world who are not fit?"

It all began to fall into place, as the cake-slicing had. New Kazos arrived every year, invariably upstanding specimens—selected, it seemed, by the human overlords of Kazo. Men like his father. No, the choices would hardly be careless, when the decisions were irrevocable and the homeworld was hostage. Even the most selfish child divided the cake fairly when any mistake applied so directly against his basic self-interest.

There would never again be the threat of war between the planets.

"The key is not so much in the system, Richard," Serena said gently, "but in the selection. Good leaders make good government—and good government breeds good leaders. I think you know from whom I learned that."

It was still too much. "Why are you telling all this to *me?*"

"Why do you think, Richard?" Bitool asked.

Then the rest of it dawned. "But I came to kill—"

"And you overcame the strongest conditioning the rebels could impose, together with your own lingering doubts," Bitool said. "Many are unable to do this. My own Fomina—"He stopped, finding that too painful even after fifteen years. "You were tempted in several ways— and did not fall. How else could we be sure of you? Surely we could not send an untempered man, no matter what his lineage. What a man believes—"

"—May be ascertained, not from his creed—" Henrys added.

"We shall not see each other again, Richard," Serena interposed sadly. "You know the secret now, and you must leave immediately."

Bitool put out his hand for an Earth-type handshake. "This has been an experience for us all, but we believe in you, Richard. Be kind to our world, Conqueror."

CHAPTER

7

◆ ◆ ◆

The rendezvous occurred in deep space. Dick Henrys had not seen an Earth ship in fifteen years, but there was no forgetting the familiar lines of the vessels that had carried his father.

Dad! Suddenly it came to him with wonderful force. His father lived! He could be with him again! And with his friend, Jon, and *his* father. . . .

The two ships came together slowly, both spinning on their long axes. After cautious maneuvering they grappled each other with flying magnets and made a nose-to-nose connection. The pseudo-gravity of each ship derived from its rotation, but Earth ships spun clockwise, Kazo ships counterclockwise, making contact hazardous. But those spins became identical when the ships met nose-to-nose, and the forward airlocks could be merged for the transfer of personnel. It was just one of the minor sophistications of interworld contact.

"As you board that ship, you become Conquerors," the Kazo officer said gravely.

Henrys nodded with the others, his heart pounding. This space adventure had come upon him with appalling suddenness. To think that he had been ready to revolt against the overlords—and now this! He could tell by the attitude of the other men that they shared his emotion.

There were better than fifty in all. Just a typical shipment, one of perhaps twenty exchanges made each year.

They stood in a line as the locks pressured. Here in the nose the way was uphill because of the narrowing of the ship, and weight was less. It seemed symbolic: they would ascend from serf-status to master-status as they climbed to the lock and stepped through that invisible gravity line.

The Kazo stood by the lock as it opened. Actually he was in the null-gray region, holding on, but his form remained militarily stiff. A human officer appeared beyond. The two reached across and shook hands formally, then moved back. The Kazo gestured, and the first human recruit climbed up and waited.

In a moment a young male Kazo passed over from the other ship. The first human recruit, briefed for this small but significant ceremony, saluted. "Overlord," he said.

The Kazo acknowledged, a bit startled. Then the human passed into the other ship, swinging himself along by the handholds. "Conqueror!" the leading Kazo recruit in that line said to him. Henrys could only see the back of the man's head, but he looked startled, too.

They completed the ceremonial transfer. Henrys saluted, and was saluted, feeling an indefinable emotion: victory and disappointment combined with the falling sensation of the weight-free passage through the locks. It was too new, too new. But now he and the others were human masters aboard a human ship. The locks closed and depressured, and the ships separated. Done!

The human captain assembled the men in the main chamber for orientation. It was crowded, for no compartment of a spaceship was large by planetary standards. "Men—brace yourselves," the captain said gravely. "You are not going to Kazo."

Dick froze. This whole elaborate exchange—had it been phony? A way to eliminate dissidents and keep Earth passive? He knew that the other young men—active, strong-willed individualists like himself—were similarly chagrined.

The captain read their faces. "No, you have not been betrayed. The system is as you have been informed. Your Kazo government selected you in good faith. But there has been a change. A third world is joining the network."

The cake was being divided three ways! Henrys had not anticipated this—but the system that worked so well for two should work for three.

"You'll acquire the details in the next few weeks," the captain continued after another pause. "This is merely a preliminary survey. We—Kazo and Earth—maintain full-strength fleets in space, for exploration and mutual protection. One of our forays encountered an alien sphere of warlike disposition. But the massed resources of Earth and Kazo exceeded those of the third world, and the merged technologies of our combine give us a special advantage. So the Ukes were disposed to negotiate." He smiled—the smile a military man would make when he knew he dealt from strength.

There was a murmur of comprehension. "If you can't beat 'em—" someone muttered.

"We showed them the advantage of our system," the captain continued. "Both Earth and Kazo have gained tremendously in the past fifteen years. In fact, had we not done so, we would not now have the advantage over Uke. Their observers recognized this. So yes—Uke is ready to participate."

A recruit raised his hand. "Sir—"

"Call me Conqueror Smith; best to get into the habit immediately," the captain said, nodding. "All Conquerors are officers by definition."

"Conqueror Smith, sir—"

"Delete the 'sir'! You're going to ask how we can trust them, right? When they're new to the system, and are perhaps joining under duress."

The recruit nodded, and so did several of the others.

"Anyone have the answer to that?" Smith asked, looking about.

Henrys raised his hand. "Conqueror, the system itself takes care of the trust. It is like dividing cake fairly—"

"You're Henrys, aren't you?"

Surprised, Henrys nodded.

"I was a crewman aboard your father's ship, fifteen years ago. Admiral Henrys is the present chief Conqueror of Kazo. His accession was extremely popular among the natives. I thought I recognized the family resemblance. And the thinking."

The others turned toward Henrys, impressed. But he plowed ahead with his answer. "It is dangerous to be sincere unless you are also stupid," he said, quoting from *The Revolutionist's Handbook*. Then he elaborated on his own. "But when the system takes insincere, selfish individual motivations into account, trust becomes implicit. If we govern Uke, and Uke governs Kazo, and Kazo governs Earth—"

Smith interrupted him again. "I have not told you that, recruit."

Still Henrys would not be moved. "Obviously you are being transferred from Kazo to Uke, Conqueror. But you are still delivering Kazo recruits to Earth. So it has to be planet Kazo that is changing governments."

The captain addressed the others. "You can see why this man's father rose to the top job. And it's no nepotism; the Kazos selected this recruit. Anyone else care to finish the reasoning?"

Several others were ready now. The captain called on one.

"If Uke governs Kazo, and Kazo governs Uke," the recruit said carefully, "then it would be self-defeating for Uke to introduce inferior representatives into the system. Bad government on Kazo would lead to bad government on Earth, and come full-circle back to Uke. So their initial complement, consisting of their entire spacefleet, will be exceedingly careful. After that, *we'll* be doing the selection on Uke, so we know the choices will be good. It's foolproof!"

Well enough stated, Dick thought. But hearing his theses from another mouth, not as the rantings of a rebel but as establishment doctrine, made him feel abruptly uncertain.

Foolproof? *Nothing* was foolproof! His whole life had been fraught with accident and error, from a mother who had married against *her* mother's preference, and a father who stayed too much in space, to an alien conquest of Earth that wasn't really a conquest, the death of his father that was instead a promotion to Conqueror status, and revolution that wasn't . . . and now his assignment to planet Kazo—that turned out to be duty on planet Uke, that he had never heard of before this hour. What certainties remained for him—except further *un*certainties? Only a fool would think of the future as foolproof.

But another question jolted him out of it. "Why are there no women?" a recruit asked.

Smith frowned. "It is the start of occupation—just as it was fifteen years ago on Earth and Kazo. There will be special dangers. We can't risk . . ."

Nonsense, Henrys thought. The medieval ages were long gone; women were no longer to be considered weak creatures to be protected. The real meaning was that men could not afford to be distracted by romantic dalliances when a world was in the throes of pacification. And the natives would assume that the occupation was temporary, so long as there were no human women.

But they had not expected female company on Kazo, either, so it was not really a disappointment. Occupation was, indeed, hazardous duty. The leaders of Uke had agreed to the method of dividing the cake—but the populace would hardly appreciate it. Any more than young Dick Henrys had appreciated the Kazo overlordship of Earth.

He would remember that: what it felt like to be the conquered. As an overlord he would have compassion, but no illusions about the motives of subject people. Bitool had taken unreasonable chances, or so it seemed in retrospect.

The occupation of Uke had been in process for several months, actually. Henrys was glad he hadn't had to participate in the initial "conquest." By this time the natives were well aware of the situation—that part of it they were permitted to know—if not resigned to it. The atmospheric pacification program was well under way, making it easier. Specific assignments were waiting for all the recruits. These were minor posts, of course; the experienced crew transferred from Kazo headed the overlord hierarchy. But Henrys knew that advancement would be rapid, because the transferees had been on a similar mission for fifteen years, and in the Space Service for up to twenty years preceding that. Like his father. Men ranging from thirty-six to fifty-six years old—no younger and no older, because of the age-regulations of the Space Service at the time of the Kazo encounter. And only half had transferred; the rest remained on Kazo to break in the Uke occupation force. A ticklish program there surely. He wondered how his father was handling it.

In the course of the next fifteen years virtually all the original overlords on all three planets would pass, and affairs would be entirely in the hands of the selectees. But the job would be harder on Uke, because this conquest was newer. The rough edges still had to be knocked off.

Uke, as seen from space, was very like Earth. This was hardly surprising, he realized. Few details of any habitable planet were visible from space. Also, the gravity, atmosphere, climate, and vegetation had to be similar, or the exchange of personnel could not take place.

What would happen if they encountered a spacefaring species whose residential environment was hostile to man or Kazo? How would that planet be integrated into the network? Surely interplanetary war remained unthinkable—but the problem of interspecies trust would remain. A bomb from a completely alien species would do as much damage as a native product.

The Ukes were little green men. Literally. Scarcely five feet tall and glossy green all over. Their arms were long, their legs short, and they had suckers at the extremities so that they could walk four-footed on walls with ease. Their elbows were marvelous joints that bent four ways. Their sensory organs, like man's, were clustered about the brain, but the proportions differed enough to make them seem like caricatures of the human countenance. They had a nest of tentacles about the mouth, making male and female seem bearded. Someone had disparagingly dubbed them "Ukeleles," though this term was forbidden on the planet.

Henrys was appalled at first. Was this the company he would have for the rest of his life? But he reminded himself that these were advanced technological people, with atomic-powered spacecraft just about as good as Earth's; they deserved the respect due to equals. And he remembered how strange the blue Kazos had seemed at first—and how quickly they had come to appear normal, and even superior.

Private briefings were scheduled from the moment the crew of recruits landed. Five Conquerors transferred from Kazo held sessions of one hour apiece with each of the fifty novices. Henrys' briefing was in the last group, but he was not permitted to step out among the natives prior to that. So he had nine hours to kill, drilling in the language of Uke. This was facilitated by high-intensity semihypnotic teaching machines, but remained a real headache to assimilate.

At last his hour came. Henrys entered the designated office. A smart young officer sat at a desk, bearing a trim moustache and beard.

Henrys stood at attention and saluted. "Conqueror, I am Richard Henrys, reporting for—" He stopped, amazed.

"What did you expect, idiot?" the man demanded. "You'll have to grow one too, you know, so as not to frighten the natives."

"Jon!" Henrys cried, charging up to the desk.

"I'm glad you made it, Dick!" Jonathan Teller said, hugging him. "I hated to leave you like that back on Earth, thinking what you must've thought, but—"

"But I was too dumb to graduate, then!" Henrys finished for him. "They finally sent a Kazo female to break me in."

"I know. Serena. Who did you think routed her there, anyway? Your dad wouldn't pull a dirty trick like that!"

"You bastard!" Henrys said happily. "I was in the middle of a revolution!"

"Yes. And you'll be using your revolutionary skills here! Some of us have got out of the resistance habit, but it's fresh for you. That's why they snuck me in to talk to you, instead of the regular briefer; we've got a lot to cover."

"Jon, you're hitting me sort of fast and heavy, here! I thought I was going to help govern Uke—"

"You are, Dick, you are! But you're going to risk your fool neck infiltrating Uke revolutionary circles, too. I'll give you the conventional assignment first, then we'll work into the real mission."

"Is this the kind of briefing all the recruits get?"

"No. But they're being given real jobs that will take their full attention. You're getting a sinecure."

"Oh. So I can practice revolution on the side?"

"Right. Now pay attention to the routine. You're assigned to a coastline post in the temperate zone of the major continent. Court duty. The natives will handle all the details. The rationale is that we have to depend on the natives, because we're spread extremely thin on Uke. There are only eleven thousand humans on the planet, most of us transferred from Kazo. The native population is nearly eleven billion. That's one human overlord for every million Ukes! And the natives are familiar with their world while man is new.

"But our battle-fleet orbits the planet, and we really do have the firepower to vaporize the entire habitable shell. Our weapons are trained on their population centers. We've set the ratio of reprisal at a million to one: for every man killed on Uke by illicit means—sabotage, rebellion, or convenient accident—one million natives will die."

"God, Jon! Even on Earth it was only a hundred thousand! Why such a—"

"This isn't Earth, Dick! The Ukes are tough, smart sentients. And we're using the ratio as a means to accomplish the necessary reduction of population. We've drawn up comprehensive lists with the aid of the Uke spacefleet intelligence experts: the incompetent, the criminal, the hopelessly impoverished, the incurably ill, the unstable, the otherwise undesirable. With five or six billion to liquidate in the course of a few years, these unfit have to be the first to go."

"But the cold-blooded murder of—"

"Appalling, isn't it? I'm hardened to it, some, and the old-line Conquerors see it as nothing more than a tactical problem. How to get the grinders constructed, how to process the pulp for fertilizer, et cetera. You'll be issued tranquilizers to tide you over the first horror—but don't use more than you have to, because we want you to keep on thinking like a native. That's part of your mission."

"I'm thinking like a human being!"

"Same thing. At the outset, a dozen men were killed from ambush, despite our warnings. So we documented the manner of their murders publicly—and arrested twelve million Ukes on our list. In the course of that project, three more men died—so we took three million more. Quite a number of these disappeared just before arrest, so we made up the number from those further down the list. We achieved the full tally: fifteen million Ukes gone, in a nice pilot project. Savage, but a good lesson. So we did establish order.

"We conscripted a greater number for labor on difficult projects, such as constructing our major base and observation post in the arctic region, and for maintenance duty on former Uke space outposts. Conditions are extreme, so that a large proportion of these workers die. We're not being intentionally brutal there; it's just the logistics of the situation. It's almost impossible to create safe working conditions until the initial labors are accomplished. At least these conscriptees have a chance; those who survive their terms are allowed to live. Better than being taken for the massive Uke organ bank. What do you think of that?"

"The whole thing is an atrocity!" Henrys said. "To think that you and I could ever support—"

"Would you rather have the Ukes overrun their resources and starve, like the deer back on Earth when their predators were eliminated?"

"No, but—"

"Enforced birth control is the best long-range mechanism—but starvation was already endemic when we came. We have to bring the population down in a hurry, or our whole effort will be wasted."

Henrys sighed. "I know, Jon, I know! I just don't like being the executioner!"

Jon let that go. "Now I've given you the routine. What's left is the real business. We have reason to believe that something is fishy on Uke, and we need a good man to get into it. I'm going to give you some good histories of the planet, and some good biology texts—"

"History and biology! I don't know anything about—"

"That's why you'll have to study them, right? Give you good practice in reading Uke, too."

"You mean they haven't even been translated? This is ridiculous!"

"I'll give you a hint: look for the missing elements. There is something funny about Uke history and about Uke anatomy. The first has gaps, the second has a superfluous nerve. We think they're related to the contemporary problem."

"And from *that* I'm supposed to figure it all out?" Henrys demanded. "I'm not even familiar with the planet!"

"Precisely. Your mind has not yet become set in the Conqueror's mold. Maybe you can find what the rest of us can't."

"This is crazy, Jon! I never—"

"Crazy! I'm glad you reminded me! There's something crazy about the Uke language, too. It's universal; everyone on the planet speaks one tongue. But there are words the Ukes themselves don't understand—"

"In their own language? That *is* crazy!"

"So you'd better try to integrate that, too. The main ghost word is 'mngh'—and it has to *have* a meaning, because it is used in their writings. But no one knows that meaning."

"Mngh," Henrys said, trying to duplicate the peculiar sound Jon had made. "I'm beginning to be intrigued."

Jon stood. "We won't be seeing each other often; I work on another continent. You'll be pretty much on your own."

"I always am!" Henrys laughed, shaking hands.

CHAPTER

8

◆ ◆ ◆

Midway through Henrys' adjustment period he received
a letter from Earth. He grasped it with fevered relief;
anything to take his mind off this horror that was Uke
language, Uke genocide, and the mysterious subversion
he was supposed to ferret out.

It was from Serena.

> Dear Richard,
> I know it is not proper to say this so soon,
> but since I will not see you again, I am com-
> pelled. Fomina was Bitool's beloved, but when
> she thought him dead her attachment fastened
> on the one closest to him in death. It is the
> way of Kazo, though we seldom speak of it.
> She killed herself for that reason; my presence
> was only the pretext. So I feel no personal
> guilt, though I regret the situation.

ᐧ Henrys paused. This was hardly a conventional well-
wishing. No preliminary remarks, no apologies; just a
straight businesslike analysis of something that concerned
him only remotely. Kazos *were* different from humans.

> For me, the loss was of my parents, who
> were surplus. I came to Conqueror Henrys
> through Fomina's intercession, but it was he
> who raised me to maturity. I was about the age
> of his lost son, apart from the minor distinc-

101

tions of planetary chronologies, and I think he
felt a certain need to complete the job correctly. Yet there was much he did not understand. He was the instrument of human policy
on planet Kazo, and so the closest to the
demise of my parents; I had to orient on him.
Like Fomina, I recognized in him elements I
required, though he was alien. She had oriented
on him as mate, and died of the essential conflict; I do not think he ever realized that, for
he saw her only as Bitool's bereaved. I oriented
on him as parent. That he could accept, so I
succeeded in the adjustment; but it was a thing
of a difficulty you may not be equipped to
appreciate.

He had to break off the reading again. He tried to
imagine adopting a Kazo father. Bitool . . . yes, he
thought he was equipped to appreciate it. But still: why
was Serena telling him all this now? Obviously she had
come through it all right—in fact, very well, for now she
was among the first of her sex to make the transfer between worlds.

When I came into contact with a human
male of my own generation, suffering the same
hurts I had suffered, yet bearing my bene-
factor's name and many of his characteristics,
I began to comprehend the extent of Fomina's
dilemma. My reservations about the Conqueror
had almost entirely broken down, owing to the
years of proximity to a human of fine qualities
and the more recent shock of transfer into
overlord status. What I did in that time of
adjustment was not really the temptation of a
candidate for transfer, but an expression of my
own confused yearnings. A Kazo female does
not make an offer such as I made to you in
innocence, Richard. We do comprehend the
meaning of sex.

> Fortunately we are now apart, and other
> men of your species do not have the same
> effect upon me. Please do not take offense: I
> feel about you as Fomina felt about your
> father, but I shall not die of it. I love you.

Henrys struggled with the letter, unwilling to comprehend its plain statement. The horror of the human policy on Uke merged with the shock of the letter, making him uncertain whether he objected more to genocide or to miscegenation. But it did show him that he remained emotionally vulnerable on more than one front; and that, oddly, seemed to help him to get over both.

The court was elegant. Columns that were trapezoidal in cross-section supported the sculptured ceiling. The material of walls and floor amplified the words spoken anywhere in the room, but gently, so that the speaker seemed near.

Henrys had the place of honor above and behind the Uke judge's desk. He did not handle the ritual of trial; he merely oversaw it. The judge took care of the details. Henrys had no robe or insignia of rank. He was a man, and that made his authority absolute.

He knew this court assignment was a minor one, theoretically intended to give him practice in the supervision of intelligent natives. He also knew his real job was elsewhere, as he studied Uke language and history and anatomy. But he resolved to do the best job he could, coming to grips with the reality of human policy on this planet, for nothing was minor where lives were concerned.

The first native stepped up before the judgment desk. Henrys touched a button, and a page of specifics appeared on his monitor screen in Uke print. It was a strain to read it, and he longed for a translation—but English was a secret language here.

"Case #1: theft. SUMMARY: took loaf of gunkel bread from counter, consumed same during chase." He wasn't sure he had every word right, but that was close enough.

Henrys pushed a second button and got the detail documentation: how the accused had lingered without buying, arousing the proprietor's suspicion; had snatched the loaf when another customer blocked the view of that section of the counter momentarily; run while attempting to conceal the loaf; eaten it while in motion as the police closed in; surrendered without resistance thereafter.

There were statements from the proprietor, the other customer, the policeuke, and two incidental witnesses. Query: "Why did you do it?" Answer: "I was hungry." Physician's report: "Accused shows overt symptoms of malnutrition." Welfare board's report: "Accused, being able-bodied, is not eligible for state assistance." Employment office's report: "Accused is not sufficiently trained for sophisticated position. A ukepower surplus exists on the menial-task level. Earliest employment opportunity: five months after application."

So the accused had been out of work and hungry. His society had offered him no opportunity to better himself —or perhaps he had had opportunity and squandered it. He had either to starve—or steal food.

Henrys pushed the third button. The words appeared: "RECOMMENDATION: oblivion."

The Uke judge was waiting for Henrys' reaction. There were many more cases to process this day; they had to average about one a minute if the court was not to run overtime. He had either to intercede—or allow the accused to enter the death chamber.

It was a clear-cut case, and the plea was "Guilty." And the population had to be halved rapidly. The accused was obviously an incompetent: unwilling or unable to obtain the qualifications required for a position not already glutted by applicants. The Earth government had made training and placement available to all but forced no native into any particular slot. Was he now to spare the accused, invoking state aid for his support—at the sacrifice of some other native's life? This was not the occasion for niceness or human emotion; this required objectivity. The best interests of the planet dictated that the accused be written off.

Henrys' heart was pounding, but he pushed the fourth button and spoke carefully in Ukish. His voice would be audible to the entire assembly. "Recommendation approved. All recommendations shall be considered approved unless I specifically intercede. Proceed at a convenient pace."

There it was: blanket approval. Henrys could sleep on the job, literally, and the trials would continue without a hitch. He did not have to acquaint himself with the morbid details. If such decisions of death hurt, he could wash his hands of them.

It was also a seeming invitation to native corruption.

The second case came up. He pressed the first button for the summary: "Curfew violation. Accused was walking the streets beyond his warren when apprehended." The documentation established the specific time and locale, and the accused's given excuse: he had forgotten the time. That was phony, as the time of curfew was dusk; no one could miss it. The recommendation was oblivion, and Henrys let it stand.

So the second Uke approached the door of death. He balked, clinging to the floor with his suckers. The doorguard lowered his needlepoint spear and punctured the pads: one, two, three, four. Now the accused was unable to hold fast to any surface, and was boosted through. The entire sequence, from start of trial to closure of door, had taken only forty-five seconds.

Case #3 concerned the interference of the rights of others. Specifically, the accused had extended his warren apartment five inches into the access hall, in order to accommodate a larger television screen. This interfered with normal passage, as the hall was just large enough for the traffic it bore. A neighbor had complained, and the police had investigated. Recommendation: oblivion.

Henrys stayed out of it. He had little sympathy with the asocial attitude betrayed here. The accused had understood the need for free access to every section of the crowded warren, but had placed his own convenience above that of many others. He could be dispensed with.

Five hundred cases passed through that court the first day. Henrys interfered with none. The Uke apparatus had done its work well, making every case a model of clarity. Four hundred and ninety-seven resulted in oblivion; two were remanded by the Uke judge for further study; one was acquitted owing to a technical error in the case. The standard penalty was harsh—but this was a working method to reduce the population, and the trials were fast and fair. If the malingerers and thieves were spared, honest citizens would eventually be taken. And it encouraged strict adherence to the law.

Henrys took his pacifier so that he could sleep that night. Even so he dreamed of an endless line of green men going to the guillotine, their heads rolling, rolling. . . .

On the second day he oversaw another quota of five hundred cases without interceding. But he was not sleeping. He was watching for something.

On the third day he knew the court had largely forgotten he was there. The first sign of what he waited for would be minor. He scrutinized each case carefully, though he sat so still that the Uke judge might think he was snoozing. And all this reading was excellent practice in the language.

Case #335 for the day: Disrespectful remark about overlords.

Henrys snapped alert. He had almost missed it, amid the monotony of a case a minute. He punched for documentation: a summary of a recording of the accused's statement. "Conquerors are homosexual because they have no women." Recommendation: oblivion.

Quickly he checked the complete statement in context. "If I had to serve duty offplanet without females of my own kind for the rest of my life, I'd be tempted to turn homosexual. I'm sure the Conquerors have similar temptations."

The accused was heading for the door. He had to; resistance in court would not save him, and the penalty for that would be trial of all his family. Guilt by association was valid in a case like this.

Henrys pushed the fourth button. "Accused pause," he said quietly.

His word electrified the court. All green heads turned toward the projectile-proof plastic that shielded him, and the accused froze in place.

"Judge will read detail specification aloud to court," Henrys said.

The judge read the full quotation.

"Reconsider verdict," Henrys said.

"Conqueror Henrys has interceded," the judge said immediately. "Case dismissed."

"No," Henrys said softly. "I have not interceded. This Uke must be tried fairly. Reconsider verdict."

"Evidence insufficient," the judge said. "Accused will be held for retrial—"

"No," Henrys repeated. There was a murmur in the courtroom that was silenced instantly as he glanced up. The accused remained immobile.

"What is it you wish, Conqueror?" the judge asked, baffled.

"Clerk," Henrys said. The Uke addressed sprang to attention, his suckers popping with the force of his motion. "Draw up a specification for the trial of this judge. Charge: inattention to detail prejudicial to proper procedure of this court. Charge the functionary responsible for the summary of Case #335 this date similarly."

The clerk held his noteboard to his face and used his mouth tentacles to scribble the specification in his own script. Two guards came up bearing an arrest-hoop and placed it about the judge's torso. A replacement judge took the bench.

Henrys turned to the accused. "Did you make the statement?"

"Yes, Conqueror."

"Then why did you plead 'not guilty' to the specification?"

"My statement was not intended disrespectfully, Conqueror."

"Yet the implication is clear enough, and conducive to contempt for human beings."

"Yes, Conqueror."

"Don't 'yes Conqueror' me when I misstate the case!" Henrys roared. "*You* may die—but your relatives shall be spared so long as you respond honestly. Do not tell me what you think I want to hear; speak the truth as you understand it."

The Uke stared, his mouth tentacles wriggling. "Conqueror," he said, faltering. "I—I speak as directed. My statement was made privately, and merely reflected the-the contempt that already exists. I-I was actually attempting to *explain* it. My meaning was that the *situation* of the Conquerors on our planet is conducive to temptation. I did not say they—you would yield to it."

"Not when contact between Conquerors is restricted to occasional administrative contacts, publicly conducted," Henrys said. "The real temptation would be interspecies miscegenation—relations between Conquerors and Uke-native females. Opportunity exists there."

The accused nodded. "Yes, Conqueror."

Suddenly Henrys realized what he had said. How close it was to what Serena had implied in her letter!

"Would you petition the government to import human females?" Henrys asked, knowing that this would shake up the Ukes just as the importation of the first Kazo female to Earth had shaken *him* up. Colonization!

"I would prefer to have you go home to your own planet, Conqueror."

Henrys smiled, stroking the stubby beard he was growing. "And I would prefer to oblige you. But we are doing a necessary job here—a job you will appreciate in later years. Meanwhile, I can set one speculation at rest. All Conquerors on duty here are required to take medication suppressing the sexual functions. There is therefore little temptation either to homosexuality or miscegenation. Were you assigned to offplanet duty, you would be similarly

dosed, instead of merely having your fertility reduced."
Henrys turned to the larger court. "A person's private
statement of opinion is not in itself disrespectful, particularly when based on commonly known facts. The accused
identified a legitimate potential problem, as he has a right
to do. We hope in the course of our government of Uke to
promote complete freedom of opinion in speech and print;
this is one of the rights of the individual that humans support. The accused's statement was recorded without his
permission, and then inaccurately summarized. This was a
double infringement of his rights. I have not interceded on
his behalf; I have interceded to prevent mistrial. He shall
be retried by another court with the proceedings of *this*
trial entered in evidence. Judge—next case."

Henrys knew he had saved a life. But he had also acted
to enhance native respect for his court. It would be a long
time before another clerk attempted to slip by an inaccurate summary. And the new judge would be alert to catch
any such errors. An emotional issue would not soon again
be fed into this court, testing the reflexes of the presiding
Conqueror.

But he made a private note for the other court, advising
the Conqueror in charge to have this particular Uke
watched after he was freed. Something useful might come
of it.

The grind of cases continued. The parade of accused
passed through the final door, and Henrys, despite his
horror of the process, gradually became acclimatized. He
had told himself many times that these same Ukes might
even now be dying far more miserably of disease and
starvation and war, if the human government had not
come to put the planet in order—and now he was beginning
to believe it, emotionally as well as intellectually. As it was,
the best representatives of the species would survive, and
the animal and plant life of the planet would also survive,
in far better comfort and security than would otherwise
have been possible.

He completed his studies of language, history, and
anatomy. A pattern began to form, linking the mysterious

nerve leading to the Uke brain with the term "mngh" and perhaps with the oddities of Uke history. Then he had a lead into what just might be the critical breakthrough—but it seemed so farfetched that he made no report to Jon or his superiors.

> Dear Serena,
> It has been a difficult adjustment. I have been installed as the supervisor to a court. All I do is oversee the cases, and intervene if I spot any error. I don't like the work, but I know it is my apprenticeship; I have to demonstrate competence in routine work before being given responsibility for policy.

So far, so good. He had to be careful what he wrote to her, because probably she didn't know that he had gone to a third world instead of Kazo. He wasn't going to lie to her, but he had to make it general enough so that the censor wouldn't bounce the letter back.

Also, he didn't know how to comment directly on her own letter—but he had to answer it. So he tried to change the subject.

> One day I caught an inaccurate summary that unfairly convicted the accused. The judge didn't understand my objection, so I had *him* put on trial. In retrospect I think I was too rough on him; it was the first exercise of my new power, and maybe it went to my head. I hate this necessity of assembly-line justice.
> Ten days later I caught another suspicious case. The charge was breach of commitment to mate. Only the female's statement was offered in evidence. I had it thrown back for further investigation, and it turned out to be a frame-up. You females are always trying to—

Oh-oh! She would be certain to take that the wrong way. And maybe they no longer had such trials on planet Kazo.

Why couldn't the truth—all of it—be made known? This double network of secrecy was a menace.

So delete the last paragraph, and resume:

> I had the native I had saved watched. We checked the identities of all others he had contact with, and analyzed the pattern on the computer. Most were legitimate—relatives and friends. But one stranger to his prior situation showed up—and when we ran a pattern on *that* one, we found it highly suspicious. We arrested him—and lo! he was no native at all, but a Kazo spy with forged identity, named Nuxto.

Oops! He had flubbed it again. Well, he would have to throw out this entire letter. So to hell with the secrecy!

> Seems your species is keeping track of ours. Nuxto looked just like a native, but of course he couldn't duplicate all the Uke's special abilities, like walking on ceilings. We let him go— but I told him to keep an eye on me, because anything I might uncover would have just as much relevance to his world, that the Ukes now govern, as to Earth. I'm sure he will.
>
> Our wider pattern analysis also turned up the first real break of my secret mission. We discovered a nonperson named Pfo. Possibly this is one of the Ukes slain by the native government just before we conquered the planet. That is, listed killed, but actually still functioning under a new, unlisted identity. Great numbers may have disappeared that way. But the whole thing is still too farfetched to present as fact, so I'll have to check it out on my own. Since this may be dangerous, I want to tell you that

He tore up the letter and burned it. He could not afford to advertise his true mission in any form. He had not even contacted Jon about it. Between the necessary secrecy and his own uncertainty—well, it was time to get some direct information.

New letter:

> Dear Serena,
> We too have conventions. My father raised you; you are my sister. I love you too.

This one he mailed. Then he went out on what he was afraid was either a wild-goose chase or a suicide mission; perhaps both. This seemed to be the proper time for it.

CHAPTER

9

◆ ◆ ◆

It wa a run-down neighborhood, similar in essence if not detail to many on Earth. Uke children scurried agilely on their four-way joints, disappearing into the wormholes of the towering termite-tenement that was a major warren. Their little feet and hands clung to the bare surface, suction cups letting go without a sound. On level ground a man could handily outdistance the swiftest Uke, but on a glossy incline the advantage shifted, and no man could match a Uke on the vertical.

Henrys knew his presence here was causing a stir. Any native could drop a strangle-wire over his head and kill him in seconds. There would be many who would want to, for this district had been decimated since the human occupation. Thousands had passed through his own court to oblivion: his face and form were well known despite his recency of arrival. But he also knew that fear, once thoroughly instilled, was extremely difficult to overcome. The sight of a man chilled the average Uke, as the sight of the hooded executioner chilled the old-time criminals of Earth. Most natives would flee him, and the more sensible members of the community would restrain the hotheads. There was an element of risk in his walking here alone— but one million Uke lives were hostage for his life, minimizing that risk.

And it was nothing compared to what he was about to do.

A Uke adult emerged from a tunnel. Male, uniformed: a keeper of order. "Lord," the policeuke said.

"I seek Pfo," Henrys said, naming the name the Conquerors were not supposed to know.

"I misunderstand," the Uke said after a pause. "What is the number?"

"Pfo has no legal identity; you know that. I wish only to talk. No arrest."

There was another pained pause. The Uke could not afford to insult the Conqueror by denying him, but to accede was to confirm Pfo's presence in this warren. "I shall bring one better informed than I to speak with you."

"No. Take me to Pfo." If he let the Ukes consult, they would find some way to balk him. He had to use his advantage of surprise and push through to victory.

"Lord, the warren is not suited!"

Henrys had some notion of native protocol when an envoy came to an enemy warren. "I stand on green blood, though my blood is red. Bind me and blind me and take me, or I depart with grievance. Our talk shall be unrecorded." He held out a green cloth and a length of cord, for the binding and blinding. The oath of green blood could not be debated—if they accepted it from an alien.

"Lord! Even so, your life—"

"Am I known as an unscrupulous man? Surely Pfo is honorable!"

"It is a region beyond honor!"

"But not beyond self-interest."

"If you die, the warren may be leveled."

"Yes. So it would seem easier merely to talk."

Henrys waited. He remembered how Serena had trusted herself to a professed rebel amid an armed revolution. Trust was powerfully conducive, as were courage and integrity. Uke values differed from those of Earth, but not that much.

The Uke tied the cloth about his head and looped a token length of cord about his body. The native's suckers were not useful for this, so the knotting was done by the mouth feelers, far more flexible than man's fingers. Many Ukes gathered about, their anonymity now protected. Henrys was gently lifted in some kind of sling and carried; again, the suckers could not grasp him directly, but could hold the plastic tags attached to the cords.

He could trace his progress somewhat by the motions, and by the sounds of other activities and their echoes. Down the narrow alley, up a narrower ramp—and then, by the alarming feel of it, across the vertical face of the warren. How high were they? If the Ukes slipped—

Then into a high tunnel. Through several small chambers, up and down curved passages. A halt. "Lord, we must search your person."

"As you will," Henrys said. Sucker-pads ran over his body, marvelously flexible and a trifle greasy, exploring every part of his clothing.

"Fluoro," the voice said. Henrys nodded. The fluoroscope would show that he concealed nothing inside his body.

"The jaw—" the Uke said.

He had forgotten! "Deterioration of several teeth during childhood. Metallic reconstruction. Inert."

"Detonator beam?"

They *were* being thorough. A Uke detonator beam would set off almost any metallic explosive and foul up any diode-type device. If he *had* primed his teeth for weaponry or radio communication, the experience would have been extremely uncomfortable. But he nodded affirmatively.

It was no bluff. He recognized the trace warmth of the beam's traverse through his jaw, and his teeth ached momentarily. They must have accepted his green-blood oath, for possession of the detonator was illegal. He was pledged not to betray that secret, and he would not—but it verified that he was on the right track.

"Null," their technician murmured.

The bearers picked him up again, still blinded. He had passed inspection.

Later, they seemed to be walking along the ceiling, suspending him below. Surely this was deep within the warren, and virtually impassable to human beings. Spelunkers might navigate the buried passages—but it would be extremely hazardous in the face of native resistance, even without having to get around such sophisticated items as a detonator-beam projector. In fact, the only way really to comprehend the depths of a warren would be to gas it, knocking out all the denizens, then send in a skilled charting team. At present the government was dependent on native maps—which could be inaccurate.

At length they set him down and removed the ties and blindfold. Henrys had visualized a cavern of sorts, but this was a completely modern Uke apartment. Small trapezoidal rods extended from floor to ceiling, and cooking and feeding equipment was stuck to one wall by little imitation-Uke-foot suckers. Clothing decorated another wall, and a third wall was library: books whose thin plastic sheets were folded accordion-style, or like old Earth road-maps, the whole bound together and suctioned to the wall in the usual fashion. But there was no electronic equipment: no television or sonic cleaner, no communications apparatus. Gas lamps illuminated the room, and there was a water pump. So it was not really so modern as he had thought at first.

There would be no power drain from this apartment. Thus no billing and no registry. The complex network of the warren, which might contain as many as a million individual apartments, *not* arranged symmetrically, was unmappable, really. No one could identify this room unless the Uke charts carried it—and Henrys was sure they didn't. His host was nonexistent.

All this observation was peripheral as Henrys appraised the proprietor. Pfo was a young male Uke in good health. His skin was an almost glossy green and he possessed the assurance of the born revolutionist. Henrys was reminded of himself of only a year or two before—and perhaps not so long ago as that. There was a type . . .

"Conqueror intelligence is better than we had supposed," Pfo remarked, speaking slowly and pronouncing his words precisely on the assumption that Henrys had difficulty understanding him. "Yet I see no reason for you to have exposed yourself in this manner." His mouth-tentacles coiled into the Uke equivalent of question marks.

Henrys shrugged. "Perhaps my assumptions differ from yours. May we speak freely here?"

"That depends on the nature of the speech."

"It is treasonous."

The tentacles vibrated with humor. "Treason we must speak elsewhere."

Henrys wished his beard were that expressive. "Summon your carriers, then."

"No." Pfo studied him frankly. "I know your record in the court. You are fair, but you would not betray your kind. Neither will I betray mine. We cannot compromise, so speech is pointless."

Henrys smiled. He like this rebel—as he had expected to. "There may be a standard superseding species loyalty."

"The carriers will conduct you to the street."

Henrys sat down on the floor. "I shall not go."

The Uke paused, as well he might. Henrys had just raised the specter of one million executions. "This does not conform to green blood."

"The violation is yours. I came to talk—you refuse."

Pfo jumped to the ceiling, startling Henrys. The Uke reached into the hole above and brought down a rope. It dangled, suspended from a tie somewhere out of sight. "Your grip is adequate?"

"Let me knot it." Henrys took the dangling end and formed a stout knot. He hefted himself to sit on that, clenching his thighs while his hands held on higher up. The rope was smooth plastic, suitable for Uke suckers to grasp.

It lifted. Henrys had to pull his body in tight to avoid swinging into the ceiling rim as his head entered the hole. Then it was dark, except for the light below.

He swung across a stony partition, then could see nothing. The rope dropped suddenly—and far. He was plunging down a vertical shaft, ten, twenty, thirty feet and more. There was no light at all, and the air smelled dank.

The rope quivered, swung again, dropped again. He wondered what mechanism enabled it to move like this, for there could not be much room in such a shaft, and the rope could not be of indefinite length. Probably a system of clamp-on friction pulleys: when the limit of extension was reached, a new pulley would attach to the lower reaches, just above him, and guide him down another stretch. Primitive but sophisticated. And still no electric power required.

At last his feet touched rock in the dark. He let go and stood, glad to relieve his cramped hand and bruised thighs.

"This way," Pfo's voice said in the blackness.

Henrys followed. He might as well have been blind-folded. They passed around two sharp corners, and there was light: another gas lamp, set low. But this was no apartment; the walls were bare and slick with moisture, and the air was cold.

"Now talk," Pfo said. "I only listen."

"Sixteen years ago," Henrys said, ignoring planetary distinctions, "planet Earth was conquered by an alien species. It never threw off that yoke."

Pfo, who may have thought he was prepared for anything, wasn't. The Uke's tentacles went stiff and his joints flexed in his equivalent of a dropped jaw.

Henrys knew the feeling. And now he knew Pfo was not party to the cake division. The Uke was a true rev-olutionist, not a traitor to the agreed system. That was good.

"I was a revolutionist, like you," Henrys said. This was his treason: he was telling a native the truth. The Ukes were supposed to believe that there was no recourse ex-cept cooperation with the Conquerors; otherwise they might attempt to subvert the system. "But I discovered that my revolt was futile, because success would have been far more costly than failure. Even my revolution was counterfeit—as is yours."

Pfo had recovered from his first shock. "I admit to no revolution. I am sure yours *was* counterfeit—for you were never conquered. Instead you conquered *my* world. Why come to me, risking your life and mine, with such fiction? There is no rationale."

"Unless I speak the truth," Henrys said.

"That Earth was conquered? That success would hurt my people more than failure?" Pfo spun his green elbow about in a little circle, hand and shoulder fixed in place: a shrug of negation and perplexity.

"Are the Conquerors unfair in their enforcement of the law?" Henrys asked.

"No. Some mistakes—but you are better than our own officials. But the penalties—"

Henrys had been through this before, on Earth. He had argued the revolutionist's case with Serena, and could just about predict the Uke's objections. "Those penalties —could order be maintained without them? Population be reduced? Poverty and starvation and illness eliminated? War prevented?"

Pfo held up a sucker in an almost human gesture. "I know all the Conqueror's arguments! I admit your tyranny seems bloody but benign—so far. But the fallacy—"

"Is that it isn't *native*," Henrys finished. "But suppose that your native government—or at least your space force —was *not* annihilated, but is governing another planet, just as we govern yours? Each doing for another world what it could not do for its own?"

Pfo, stalled in mid-argument, was silent for a time. "It is a tempting notion. But your loyalty is to your species, and naturally you seek to subvert our resistance."

"My loyalty is to the cause of justice, of peace, of universal prosperity—and continued survival for my own species and others," Henrys said. "Why should I risk my life in any lesser cause? I could have gassed this warren at no risk to myself."

Pfo walked the floor restlessly, as a man would do.

Then he walked up the wall, as a man could not. Yet how superficial were the real distinctions between species. "You question the very suction of my cause," he admitted, showing a hand-disk momentarily. Loss of suction could be fatal to a climbing Uke. "But you offer no proof. I question your word in no other respect—but to believe you in this without evidence is certainly treason!"

"I agree!" Henrys said heartily. "Now we are ready to bargain."

"No bargaining!" Pfo cried in anguish. "If you are right, I dare not oppose you. If wrong—"

Henrys saw he was getting bogged down in argument. Bitool could have handled this better. "No bargaining. I regret an inappropriate choice of words. This is merely a mutual understanding of the necessities of our positions. I shall prove to you that I am right, and your resources shall be mine. Or you shall prove to me that *you* are right, and I will die."

"One million murders in reprisal—"

"A small price to protect the future of your planet."

"But others will come after you—"

"And you will be gone as if you never were, long before they arrive." Henrys tried to spin his elbow, but failed. "Why not let your superiors decide? They may kill me anyway—but the onus will not be on you."

"I can take you to Smy. But if you convince him, why should he kill you?"

"That is for you to think about," Henrys said.

They had come to terms. "This way," Pfo said.

"No blindfold?"

"This entire level is rebel-controlled. Stay close to me, lest our assassins misunderstand."

Helpful advice. Pfo led the way along the cold, silent passages, carrying a dim lamp. These were ancient catacombs, with the advantage of being without power lead-ins and therefore opaque to the Earth government. An excellent way to travel unobserved—if one had the fortitude to walk it.

They came to a stall. Two "horses" were there: green

beasts with suckered feet and four-way joints, capable of much greater speed than the sapients. They were saddled and ready: a pony express? Pfo mounted one, his suckers adhering readily to the slick flanks. Henrys climbed aboard the other with some difficulty and inner trepidation.

His concern was well justified. The gait of the creature was like no vehicle he had ridden. Up, down, around—and the steed paid scant attention to the level. It sought the region of best purchase for its large suckers, which happened to be partway up the curving tunnel wall. Pfo rode the tilt without apparent discomfort, hardly needing the saddle, but Henrys had to hang on desperately. The passage was shooting by at a good fifteen miles per hour, and that was just comfortable cruising speed, it seemed. A peculiar feeling developed in his stomach, and after a time he recognized it as motion sickness. But he refused to yield to it, for that would not befit a Conqueror.

"Danger," Pfo said, reining his mount.

Henrys did not know how to stop his own beast, but it pulled abreast of the other and halted on its own. They waited, standing almost parallel to the floor.

"Rrwr," Pfo said.

The word was on the periphery of Henrys' comprehsion. It meant some kind of wild beast, the equivalent of an Earthly tiger or bear. Most of the wild animals of Uke's golden age of nature were now extinct, crowded out by the dominant species, but it seemed a few remained in inhospitable regions such as this.

"It has been fed," Pfo said after a moment. "Let it pass in silence."

There was no sound, but now in the light of Pfo's lantern Henrys saw the malevolent eyes of some great beast approaching. His steed tensed into immobility, and Henrys did likewise.

The rrwr passed along the far side of the tunnel, huge and sleek, its outsize suckers clinging to the curving wall faultlessly. It had no claws, but its crossing tusks and python torso made it formidable. Its mouth tentacles were much larger than those of the civilized Ukes, capable of tremendous force. This was no tiger, no bear—but a dragon! It was obviously capable of tremendous velocity, yet was low enough to pass through fairly small-diameter tunnels. The terror of the netherworld, certainly.

It paid no attention to the waiting party. Like a big cat, it did not kill unless hungry.

"Now proceed," Pfo said at last.

"Why don't you eliminate that menace?" Henrys asked, shivering.

"There are already too few wild creatures remaining," Pfo replied. "And they are useful to keep intruders out of this region. We feed them just before we travel. Sometimes they dine on traitors."

Excellent terrorizing tactics, Henrys thought. These rebels were serious about their business.

Eventually they stopped and dismounted. Henrys felt sick and dizzy, and his limbs ached. He estimated they had come twenty miles. But he followed Pfo through further passages without complaint, wondering idly to what extent the lack of electric power in the demesnes of the revolutionists reflected on their political potential. Not much, he decided. The human government counted on its ability to stifle an entire warren by opening a single master switch—but these rebels functioned independently of electric power. A cut-off would send the natives into the streets in a near-riot—or down into the suction of the revolution. The mechanical pulleys must have lowered monstrous stores of food and equipment into this realm, ready for just that eventuality. The Conqueror's control was not nearly as secure as men had supposed.

Word had gone ahead. Did they use flashers or carrier animals for their communications? The passage opened into a major cavern lighted by large lamps hanging from the many-holed ceiling. Some twenty Ukes stood in the center.

"Conqueror Henrys," Pfo said to them. "He seeks to convince us that revolution is futile."

"He must die," one of the other Ukes said.

"By what authority do you decide, without hearing my case?" Henrys demanded.

"I am Smy—district leader of the revolution."

The district would include about twenty warrens, Henrys realized—roughly equivalent to the population under the jurisdiction of his court. Of course it was no coincidence that his assignment was in the center of the suspected revolutionary activity.

Henrys strode to the center, preempting the floor. "You are from the local warrens," he said. "None of your identities appear in our records." He could tell by their studied lack of reaction that his guess was accurate. "Below each warren is a rebel cell, whose leader is the only one to know the other leaders, and whose district leader is the only avenue to higher power. Few of you know your actual leadership."

He turned around, looking at each in turn. "Make certain this meeting is secure, for I am about to subvert you. No word goes outside until you send it out—for your own safety."

"He means it," Pfo said. "Our guards must not overhear the private business of the command network."

Smy considered, then made a signal. Four Ukes left the circle and went out and up into the several entrance tunnels to warn away the guards.

"You are all honest revolutionaries," Henrys said when the group was complete again. "You believe that the affairs of Uke must be restored to Uke government, for you cannot trust the motives of a foreign conqueror. But suppose you had proof that the Conquerors were more trustworthy than your own leadership? Their motives superior?"

"Our loyalty lies with our own," Smy said flatly.

"And if I show you that your leaders contemplate the same kind of planetary conquest and empire you believe Earth to be practicing now—and are using treachery to achieve it?"

"This is unprovable because it is false," Smy said. "But even then, we support our own against the alien."

Pfo, already conversant with Henrys' thesis, took issue. "No, I do not support treachery. Or empire. These are what I am fighting *against*."

"He has already subverted you!" Smy said contemptuously.

"He is honest," Pfo said. "As am I. I would support an honest Conqueror before a corrupt rebel."

"That is a contradiction in terms!" Smy said. But many of the others flexed their joints in negation. They had beliefs of their own, hard-won; they were not ready to follow blindly.

Henrys described the cake-slicing analogy and its interpretation to interplanetary government. "So you see, planet A governs B," he concluded. "B governs C. And C governs A. All three are undertaking the cruel necessities of population reduction, elimination of the unfit, and conservation of resources. But all will benefit enormously in the long run."

He was swaying them; he knew it. The simplicity of the piece of cake was a splendid thing, appealing to any intelligent mind beset by complex problems. They were mulling the notion over, savoring the taste, wanting to believe.

"He's lying!" the leader said. "He wants us to believe that all three worlds—Uke, Earth, and Kazo—voluntarily subjected themselves to alien occupation. No planet would do that. It is a ruse to create dissension in our ranks—as it is doing now!"

Pfo looked at him sharply. "What is this name— 'Kazo'?"

"The third planet! The one he claims rules Earth!"

"He never named it," Pfo said. "Did anyone hear that name before Smy mentioned it?" The others jogged their elbows negatively and coiled their mouth-tentacles. "How did *you* know it?"

Henrys recognized a windfall. He had not laid the trap deliberately, but had avoided naming Kazo as a matter of conditioning, even though he was betraying the overall situation. The Uke district leader had trapped himself—and Pfo, sharper than Henrys himself, had caught him. Beautiful!

But Smy was no easy mark. "We interrogated an overlord," he said, speaking swiftly. "Back in the first days—we captured one and got the whole story—"

"No Earthmen were captured!" Pfo said. "All died instantly!"

"That was the story we put out," Smy said. "But one was only stunned, and survived for a day. We got the whole story, then buried him in rubble and crushed him. So that his kind would think the collapse of the building had killed him outright."

The Uke leader had thought swiftly to cover his slip, as befitted one in his position—but in his haste he had betrayed himself again. Henrys let Pfo nail it.

"So Conqueror Henrys' story is *true! You* were lying, not he! Our own leadership *is* corrupt!"

Now the circle closed on the leader. Smy was a combat-hardened Uke; that was obvious. But these were tough revolutionaries who knew how to deal with betrayal wherever they found it. It was a psychology Henrys well understood.

"Fools!" Smy cried, "I lied no more than the alien! He has lived a lie during his whole stay on our world. We knew the Conqueror's secret—we merely kept it, so the humans would not suspect!"

The Ukes hesitated. "Why should our revolution give away vital information?" one asked. "The possession of information unbeknown to the enemy—"

Henrys answered now. "Earth is *not* your enemy! We kept the secret because that was a condition of the compact between the spacefleets. All agreed that premature knowledge would threaten the system. If your leaders really wanted to overthrow it, they would have spread the truth. But instead they withheld their best weapon, even from you—"

Now all the Ukes except Smy and Pfo suffered severe flexure of joints and agitation of tentacles.

"Can our own leaders be traitors?"

"The revolution is siding with Earth?"

"This is nonsense!"

"Work it out for yourselves," Henrys said. "You now know Smy lied to you. If he lied once, why not many times? Do you think he had to keep such secrets from *you,* his loyal lieutenants? Would you have given away the truth prematurely—if there were valid reason for secrecy?"

Pfo's green anger was mirrored by the others. "If there is no trust among the warren-leaders, where is the revolution?" he demanded.

"We know many things that cannot be told," Smy said. "Any one of us who enters the upper levels might be discovered, captured, tortured—or subverted." He looked meaningfully at Pfo.

Again they wavered. They were not incapable of decision; the issue was finely balanced and their minds were open. The facts were only partially visible.

Henrys plunged into his strongest effort, knowing his life was hostage. "Fine theory! But the truth is that you know your honest revolutionaries would recognize the fallacy of your position. They would see the superior system of the caké compromise for what it is, and desert the network of deceit that is the revolution. There is no reason to keep them ignorant of the facts—except the one you will not tell.

"You are maintaining both the network and the secrecy because you mean to let Earth do your dirty work —policing your planet, culling surplus population—and take the blame for its necessary cruelties. Then you will reap the benefit of both those policies you profess to detest, and the popular revulsion to them—*and still have your empire!*"

"I stand on green blood," Smy said.

The others pulled back. This was, in this circumstance, a challenge for honor—to the death. The Uke leader intended to shut him up by killing him—and the others, bound by their cultural conventions, could not interfere.

It would do no good to protest that he could prove Smy

was corrupt. He had already done that. Talk was always secondary to blood, and victory in battle always more convincing than victory in debate. He could not bypass this challenge. He had to fight.

Henrys' legs were sore from the long ride through the cold passages, and his stomach remained queasy. He was tired. But he was larger and stronger than the Uke, and should be able to prevail if the contest were fairly conducted. Perhaps this was, after all, the most expedient way.

Smy raised his arms. Two others went to search him, for it seemed weapons were not permitted. Henrys did the same, though he had been searched before. The forms had to be honored. This would probably be the only blood match ever fought between man and Uke—and the result might never be known.

Henrys had been trained in physical combat back on Earth, both with and without weapons. He had not understood why, then, for the Kazos seemed to have no reason to train their subjects in war. But he knew his ability to be imperfect, for Bitool had disarmed him easily when he came as assassin. He was no longer certain of his prowess. Which was probably a good thing.

But this was not a man he was to fight, and much of his conditioning would be useless or even disastrous. He now had considerable knowledge of Uke anatomy, of course, and it was theoretically no more difficult to subdue a Uke than a human. There were pressure points and leverages and limitations, as with the human body. But knowledge gleaned from texts might not channelize readily into the split-second decisions of physical combat.

Henrys would dispatch the Uke—or be dispatched himself. The problem was that if he eliminated Smy outright, his only avenue to the higher rebel command would be severed. He needed to trace this weed to the root, before word of his quest reached that depth. So he couldn't kill Smy, despite the license of green blood. Rather, he had to reduce the leader to such terror that he would run—back to his home base.

A tough order. Most true revolutionaries would accept honorable death before dishonorable life. Smy was a liar, and he might crack when someone like Pfo would not—but there was no guarantee. And if Henrys gave him too much leeway, the Uke might win.

Smy came at him. Perhaps he understood Henrys' position, for he showed none of the awe of the alien that Henrys had come to expect, even among these undergrounders.

He stepped aside, catching Smy's leading arm and going through the motions of a shoulder throw.

The motions did not work. The Uke joints and bending bones were quite unlike the human ones, and that changed everything. The two crashed to the floor together.

Smy sprang up immediately. His feet had remained anchored to the polished stone floor while he bent forward at the knees—a trick completely out of order for a human. It gave Smy the advantage of position, for Henrys had to scramble.

The Uke jumped. One sucker struck Henrys' head, not hard. He shook it off and stood, jabbing an elbow back. That missed too. He was glad Smy hadn't thought to pin his arm in a submission lock while he had the advantage of surprise—but of course joints were not vulnerable in the same way, on Ukes, because they bent in every direction. Smy was a creature of his conditioning too.

That soft strike to the head—what did it signify? Henrys strained to make it fit a reasonable pattern even as he spun away and kicked at his opponent's knee— ineffectively, because the knee merely bent away unhurt. The sucker to his head—of course it had not stuck, because his hair interfered with the suction. On a bald Uke head there would have been a firm connection. Then Smy could have yanked that head backward, exposing the neck . . . yes! Potentially a devasting hold. A head held captive that way could be twisted about, or bashed against the wall or floor. So Smy had tried for a punishing hold—and had failed, just as Henrys' own throw had failed. The disadvantage of reflex undermined them both.

But a skilled fighter should quickly correct for error. Surely Smy was trained, or he would not have risen to leadership, and would not have been so quick to challenge. And he thought he could prevail—with reason?

But this was hardly the time for conjecture. Henrys faced a dangerous creature—one he needed to cow, not kill. Very soon one of them would figure out a prevailing strategy of combat—and it had better be Henrys!

Throws were no good; those sticker-feet prevented them. It would be similarly hard to shove the Uke off-balance, as balance was meaningless. Arm-locks and leg-locks were out; those full-circle joints could not be locked, and the attempt would only give Smy notions to try in return. But blows and nerve attacks should be effective. Henrys, with his locking joints and one-pull muscles, was more specialized for hitting; he could strike faster and harder.

Smy had also paused for reflection. Now the Uke knew that suction was of limited value here, and that the Earthman had power to spare. What would be his new strategy?

Henrys came at Smy with his fists. The head was a weak spot in any intelligent species, because it housed the delicate brain and the soft perceptive organs. Several good knocks there—

But Smy's head flipped back on its loosely hinged neck, making the first blow ineffective. Henrys, overbalanced, fell forward. Suddenly the Uke overturned, his feet swinging up as his hands went down. Such gymnastics were easy for a creature whose touch on the floor was always a firm anchorage.

Henrys found himself on hands and knees, the Uke's body arched over him. He tried to lift—but the suckers of feet and hands pinned him down. He knew at once that he could not snap loose that grip, for it was on the floor, not his body, and any sucker could easily sustain a pull of several hundred pounds.

He dropped to his belly and tried to scramble out from under. But Smy dropped with him, holding him down more firmly. Henrys could not gain purchase in this position. He knocked at one sucker, trying to jar it loose, but the six-inch disk was leather-hard and would not budge.

Suddenly Smy released one attachment and slung his rubberlike arm about Henrys' neck. The sucker connected to Smy's own other arm, locking there. Now he had a stranglehold on a pinned man: an excellent position.

Henrys wrestled himself about to lie on his back. The strangle was not strong, because Smy had not yet tightened it, could not use his hands directly, and did not know the precise spots of vulnerability. But he would soon figure everything out.

Henrys took hold of the encircling arm with both hands. The bones were flexible, like leaf-springs in a metal suspension system; he discovered no pressure points. Even as he pulled, the grip tightened, constricting about his throat. It was getting uncomfortable.

He let go and tried a harsher measure: stiffened fingers jabbed at the eyes.

Smy's head folded back almost against his shoulders, putting his eyes out of convenient reach. But Henrys had found his avenue. He closed his fists and commenced a drumbeat of knuckle blows to the sides of Smy's head and neck. His leverage was not good, but there were nerves there; those strikes had to hurt.

The Uke let go abruptly, lifting upright with the single motion possible only for an anchored body. Henrys jumped to his feet, fists swinging again. But Smy did not wait to be hit. He scooted across the floor and up the wall.

Was he running? That was what Henrys wanted—but how could he follow? The ceiling was way out of his reach. Smy's escape would defeat Henrys' purpose much more than his death.

Henrys dived for the Uke, reaching up to catch Smy's head before it lifted entirely away. He got a fistful of mouth tentacles, but they squirmed out of his grip. One arm came down, the sucker striking Henrys' forehead— and this time it stuck. Henrys swung his fist—and struck nothing, for Smy's body was high on the wall. The second sucker-hand came down, landing over his right eye. The pad spread across nose, cheek, and eyebrow, sealing around the convolutions of his face—and stayed, because of the smooth skin and sheen of sweat on him. The air valved out through vents in the center of the sucker, making the connection tight.

Henrys knew he was in trouble. The Uke had a vacuum-grip on his eyeball.

He acted instantly. He grasped both Smy's arms with his hands and threw his entire strength into jackknifing his body upward, hanging on to the Uke. Henrys' eye was hurting as the suction hauled at it, wrenching it from the socket; he screwed it up as tightly as he could to counteract.

His feet smacked into Smy's torso as his weight jerked the other down hard. But the suckers were already letting go; had he not taken hold of Smy's arms, he would have been dropped on his back as he flipped. Or had the skin ripped off his forehead, and his eyeball popped out?

As it was, his rear smacked into the wall. But still he clung to the Uke, wrenching his body cruelly. It was not the weight so much as the angle. Smy's ankles had to bend at almost right angles while sustaining the full weight of both combatants. And now all four of Smy's appendages were accounted for: two on the wall, and two prisoned by Henrys' grip.

All this time the warren-chiefs merely watched. Henrys saw them as he swung upside down, walking his feet up the wall again to kick Smy hard in the stomach. The human form was much more superior for kicking. Five Ukes on the right, six on the left, and groups of three and four in the center. Plus one standing a little apart. Nineteen in all.

Smy was trying to haul Henrys' hands up to his mouth tentacles, but Henrys jerked and prevented that. Nineteen? There had been twenty at the outset. He had counted them automatically. Smy and nineteen others, exclusive of Pfo.

Smy let go the wall suddenly. Henrys felt the give as air rushed into the suckers through the little valves. He shoved outward with all his might. This flipped both bodies over, four feet flying in a joint cartwheel.

They struck the floor with a stunning shock, Henrys on top.

The flexible Uke body was strong for pulling and stretching, but lacked the rigid bony structure of the human torso. A crush that might have cracked a man's ribs was far more devastating to the Uke. Smy was limp. Green blood showed on his face: evidence of collapsed lungs and hydraulically burst vessels. If the Uke were not dead, it would be merciful to kill him.

"There was a spy in your number!" Henrys gasped. "One of you is missing!"

"Twel!" someone cried. "He was beside me—"

"We have to catch him!" Henrys cried, knowing the group now accepted his leadership because of the green-blood convention. "Your guards—"

"No," Pfo said. "He is out of sight. It is too late."

"Spread out in a search pattern. Cut off all exits from this region. Your planet's existence may be at stake!"

But no one moved. "This place was designed to confound pursuit," Pfo said. "All of us together could not catch any one of us, once that one had a start of a hundred paces. According to legend there are approximately thirty thousand alternate escapes—and as many hiding places or ambushes. None of us knows the entire labyrinth; it was hewn out piecemeal over millennia. Each of us knows a separate route through it, for our meetings."

Henrys slumped, knowing he had lost after all. Word of his quest was even now reaching the rebel hierarchy. Why hadn't he anticipated the spy? It was such an obvious precaution, considering the deceptive nature of the rebel command.

CHAPTER
10

◆ ◆ ◆

"Why is it so important?" Pfo asked. "They will not reveal your cake, for they already know it. And they cannot stop us from spreading the word to all the warrens —if that is your desire."

"No!" Henrys cried. "The cake must remain secret! I committed treason informing you of it, and for that I shall be tried by my own kind. But the alternative is worse."

"We will help you in any way you ask," Pfo said. "You have proved that our own leaders lied to us, and that the Conquerors mean well. You have defended it by green blood. Our revolution is over."

"No—it has just begun!" Henrys said. "If my guess is correct."

"Guess?"

"My whole mission here is based on suspicion, not certainty," Henrys said. "Some of it has been confirmed, but not enough. Your leaders will act swiftly, so you'll have to help me work out the complete truth."

"Certainly," Pfo agreed. "But what *is* it?"

"The first part I'm almost sure of—but with Smy dead, I can't prove it. So use your own judgment—no green blood on this, because I may be wrong."

Pfo spun both elbows. "You are unlike any other

Conqueror. You act with such force, yet profess uncertainty."

"Consider this: how would you set out to subvert the cake system, if you knew about it before joining?"

"I would not join it, if I did not approve it!"

"Not even if it meant having the combined war-fleets of two other planets hovering near your territory, with armament capable of incinerating your homeworld?" Henrys asked. "A force stronger than yours—and a system that refused to compromise except on its own terms?"

Several Ukes moved their joints. "I know what old King Brf would have done," one said. "Better to join—temporarily," another added.

"King Brf?"

"Our former monarch," Pfo explained. "He committed suicide with his entire retinue when the Earth fleet issued its ultimatum. Destroyed the palace and all its records."

"That was too recent for my history books," Henrys said. "I should have looked into it, as it sounds relevant. Exactly how would old King Brf have reacted—if he lived?"

"Explore the enemy's weaknesses while building our own strength," another chief said. "Until action could safely be taken. Brf was a crafty, ruthless ruler."

"Right!" Henrys cried. "But that policy requires the alien occupation of Uke. No strength could be built under those conditions."

"Let the alien occupation be only token," the Uke said. "Hide the real power out of reach of the alien. Let the Conquerors grow fat and soft in their confidence, while our people wax strong in wrath and the secret government builds up its resources—"

"Why keep it all the way underground?" Pfo demanded. "Maintain an extensive secret network whose members would not know the real—" He stopped, staring.

"Brf *lives!*" the other exclaimed. "This is exactly how he operates! Our revolution's secret leaders—"

"That's what I thought," Henrys agreed. "I once served

a revolutionary chief who was a character in an old play. At least you have a real boss."

"The king could arrange to send only picked Ukes to Kazo," Pfo continued, following the thread to its end. "Not hard to do. The Conquerors depend on Uke personnel for everything and can't even enter the warrens without our consent. We have killed many of our own, not knowing why our leaders marked them for death. If they were the ones who might honestly serve the cake—"

"Only the king's representatives could get through," the other said. "Absolutely loyal to the Conqueror— until they reach planet Kazo!"

"Thus you control two planets," Henrys said. "Your own—in all but name—and Kazo. Of course it would take a while for the human population governing Kazo to phase out, and longer to place your selected tame Kazos in the government of Earth. But in perhaps two generations you could rule all three worlds, absolutely. At no loss to yourself, except the selective culling of the weak and unfit accomplished by the Conqueror government. A net gain, really."

"*Then* throw off the yoke," Pfo said. "An empire acquired painlessly."

"Provided you maintain a powerful government in exile," Henrys said. "One that can command the loyalty of the planet. Such as the old king and all his retinue, who didn't quite manage to die in the palace explosion, and whose comprehensive records also survived. Actually, it might be better not to wait too long, because of the attrition of time; and if some revolution-oriented Conqueror became suspicious—"

"And honest revolutionaries learn that they are fostering not freedom for their world but a corrupt empire—" Pfo added.

"Brf would anticipate that," another Uke said. "He always did think deviously, leaving little to chance."

"But an early revolution—one within two or three years—would find the Conquerors still lean and strong,"

Pfo objected. He looked meaningfully at the body of Smy. "That was the district combat champion. . . ."

"And the aliens would control all electric power on the planet," the other said. "How could they be over-thrown—today?"

"That's the rest of my question," Henrys said grimly. "I agree that the move has to be made relatively soon, if only to be accomplished under the guidance of the king who inspired it. But I don't see how my government can be overthrown by force or subversion at the height of its strength. Yet King Brf must see a way."

The glance went around. All were genuinely perplexed.

"Maybe we can work this out, like the other," Henrys said, conscious of the precious time elapsing. How soon would that conspiracy strike back, acting on Twe's information? Brf would not want to let Henrys get away alive. "Are there Uke strategies of war that don't show in the texts? Frankly, aspects of your history are opaque."

"There is no understanding history," Pfo said, and it seemed the other agreed. "We have wars, empires, disasters, and blanks, following no rational pattern. Often I wonder how the present ever came about, apart from the Conquest."

"You can't make sense of your *own* history?" Henrys asked, astonished. "I thought your basic philosophies must differ from ours, so that I missed the rationale. . . ."

"Few study history, because it is nonsense," Pfo said seriously. "Mngh."

Henrys shook his head. "Mngh! Is that what it means? The inexplicable?"

"I don't know," Pfo said. "It's just an expression one uses when discussing the riddle of history and Uke nature."

Henrys would have liked to explore that further, but couldn't risk the time now. "I have only one remaining lead. Do you suppose there could be some connection to that unique Uke nerve center? It seems to have the potential to—"

"They come!" a guard shouted from one of the tunnels.

The group scattered, diving for the apertures around the cavern. Pfo climbed the wall to reach a hole in the ceiling. Henrys launched himself at the nearest tunnel his size and ran headlong down it. He ducked into the first cross passage he encountered in the sudden blackness, felt his way to an alcove, and backed into it panting.

In a moment he heard the tiniest noise, as of a Uke swinging out of an upper passage. Henrys braced himself for attack.

"No good!" the Uke whispered. "We can hear you all over the labyrinth!" It was Pfo.

"Sorry," Henrys whispered, controlling his breathing. "This just isn't my style."

"Quiet!" Pfo hissed. Then he whistled oddly. "You're the one they're after—but they're afraid your presence here is so obvious it has to be a trap. And it is; my friends are guarding the approaches."

The Uke was assuming that Henrys was the prime menace to the plan for empire. Actually, he was no menace at all—unless he figured out the missing element.

Another Uke arrived in the dark. "He's too noisy," Pfo explained in an almost inaudible whisper. "We have to get him out before they mass attack. But he can't use the walls or ceilings. We'll have to carry him."

"But that'll slow *you*—" Henrys whispered. A sucker over his mouth silenced him.

He felt cloth. Quickly he was caught up in a sling and lifted clear of the floor. What amazing lifting strength these small creatures possessed!

A light appeared. "Enemy!" Pfo said. So one had slipped through. But Henrys could now see that all the suckers of his two bearers were occupied in clinging to the ceiling. If they tried to fight, they would drop him.

The enemy made a high shrilling call, setting tentacles inside his mouth the way a human boy set two fingers. Henrys kicked out and struck him in the nest of feelers with the hard toe of his shoe. The Uke's face caved in.

Then they were up and away in the renewed blackness, climbing dizzily through a maze of crossing tunnels while the sounds of strife became loud, then faint. There was brutal maneuvering and combat going on, serving to conceal the trace noises of the escape. Henrys could feel the chill walls and small gusts of air as the configuration of his surroundings changed.

He had grossly underestimated the complexity of this honeycomb. Pfo had brought him in on the level and he hadn't paid proper attention to the tunnels leading sideways and upward. There was no need for the enemy to kill him if they wanted him silent; they had merely to isolate him here, and he would probably starve before finding his way out.

Soon they had to rest. A Uke could sustain a lot of weight in a straight pull; he knew that from his fight with Smy. But silent climbing was far more demanding, even when the load was split. The two had hauled him out of immediate danger, but they would kill themselves if they did not let up.

He did not talk. Any sound was a beacon here. It was almost impossible to locate a silent fugitive—but almost impossible to *miss* a noisy one. The biggest favor he could do his allies was to play dead, not even breathing hard.

After a time they resumed the carry, more slowly.

Several portages later they reached the edge of the labyrinth. A level, lighted hallway stretched ahead: civilization. "We should be all right here," Pfo said. "Noise no longer matters, if it is minor. You can walk."

"Just don't leave until you show me out of here," Henrys said. "This may be legitimate warren territory, but I'm completely lost."

"There is a powered elevator that will take you to the surface," Pfo told him. "This is not the warren you entered, but you will have no trouble aboveground."

"No," Henrys said abruptly. "I was letting my emotion

overrule my common sense. My mission is not complete. We have verified that corruption exists in the revolutionary network, and suspect that it is not a revolution at all but a device of undead King Brf—but we don't know where the king is hiding. More important, we don't know the *mechanism*—the way in which the human government can be overthrown today. Maybe it ties in with history or with your nervous system. I've got to *know*—and right now is my best and maybe only chance to find out."

"You have a chance to get free—and you seek more danger!" Pfo exclaimed, half in exasperation and half in admiration.

"I think they'll strike as soon as they can organize the push," Henrys said. "It may be premature for them, but they'll have no choice now, because they think the Conquerors are on to them. There'll be action within days—*and it may succeed*—unless I discover their secret weapon and defuse it."

"You are a true revolutionist," Pfo said ruefully. "But if we can't even locate their headquarters—"

"*I* don't know," Henrys said, "*You* don't know. But *they* know. What do you suppose they would do if they captured me alive?"

"Take you to the king for interrogation."

"Right! Because if it should turn out that I know nothing really important, then they can assume *you* don't know it either, and don't need to rush their preparations. But if I know everything, they'll have to make it a crash program, even if the chance of success suffers. They'll *have* to check it out—if they capture me in time."

"But the danger to you—"

"Is nothing compared to the danger to the cake! But it might be reduced if someone just happened to follow me there, and then organized a seige of the premises. . . ."

Pfo looked at the other Uke. "We'll have to use electronic tags," he snapped. "None for *him;* they'll check for that. But for the rest of us . . . the Conquerors will pick up the signals, but it doesn't matter anymore. I'll watch; you spread the word to orient on me."

The other vanished into the labyrinth.

"I hope we meet again," Henrys said, touching his fingers to Pfo's sucker. "I have enjoyed working with you." Without waiting for an answer he walked back into the dark.

At first he proceeded as quietly as he could. He didn't want it to be obvious that he was going *in*, not out. Gradually he became more careless, hefting himself noisily over ledges in the blackness, sliding down holes, running along the levels—and taking some authentic and painful tumbles. He was soon panting and tired, and that was good, because it had to seem as though he had fought his own way this far and now was lost.

A loop of cord dropped over him. Henrys grabbed it and yanked. When it didn't give, he climbed it, hand over hand.

A Uke was on the other end, of course, invisible but no doubt surprised by his reaction, and caught by the sudden heavy weight it had to sustain. Henrys found the Uke's arm, hung on, and punched his free fist at the unseen body. The native gasped and lost suction, and they both fell hard.

But now other Ukes were on him. Light flared. Henrys punched one of them in the vulnerable torso and kicked another. Then a net floated over him, entangling his arms, and in a moment he was captive.

He hoped he had made it look good enough—and that the commotion and delay had given his friends time to locate him and set up their observation system. He was glad the enemy had taken such pains to bring him in alive.

They bound him and gagged him and carried him rapidly through the darkness, just as Pfo and his companion had before. He was unable to keep track of the windings, but it hardly mattered anymore. Did he hear faint noises behind?

What if his captors realized they were being followed? Could they set traps for Pfo's forces, or dodge them? Difficult, with him hanging in this net. . . .

The lights of another warren appeared. That of the spy, Twe? How else could they be sure it was safe from the genuine revolutionists?

They boarded a shuttle—seemingly a regular warren-to-warren vehicle, electrically powered. But this was a private carriage, not a public conveyance. It had pedals set in the floor, and the light was gas. Therefore it wasn't traceable by the power monitors.

A crowd of about thirty Ukes boarded in the course of the next few minutes. This had to be the entire surviving enemy raiding party. A number were wounded, and one had lost several mouth-tentacles and was bleeding greenly. No wonder they had arrived so promptly—they had been shipped in mechanically. This underground railway was efficient.

Ukes set themselves up on the pedals, all four suckers mounted on the polished surfaces. A foreuke called the beat, and they began to pedal together. The shuttle moved —slowly, then rapidly.

Now the leader of the party removed Henrys' restraints and gag. "You are a strong fighter," the Uke said.

"And you are an able agent, Twe," Henrys said. "Tell me, now that it doesn't make any difference—was I close to the edge of that nightmare?"

"Close enough. But you were headed inward, not outward, when we caught you. You must have passed close to the edge—very close."

Henrys sighed. "I *thought* it was too long a route!"

"Your friends could have helped you, had they chosen to," Twe said. "I believe they preferred to leave you as a decoy, so that they could follow us to our lair. But my warren is secure, and their effort was for nothing."

Oh-oh! That entry to the warren balked Pfo, for there would be no concealment in that enemy territory. Unless Pfo were able to trace the route of the shuttle with his electronic sensors. . . .

The coach stopped. They dismounted and stood on a platform. The Ukes gave the vehicle a shove, and it coasted on down the track, empty. The party passed through a short tunnel and came upon another coach similar to the first.

So much for tracing the vehicle. This machine of the king's was well-oiled—and not just the shuttle. Probably the first coach would coast for miles along the slanting track, noisily, luring away the watchers.

This new coach also coasted—but in the opposite direction. It picked up speed in the dark, going down steadily. The warrens were rooted in bedrock; only the floor of the ocean was lower. Short tunnels could be cut from one low spot to another, but there would not be any extensive complex beneath the labyrinth.

But the ocean floor had been surveyed. It was all natural. So where could they be going? Surely not far, for the attack had followed Twe's escape by less than half an hour. A radioed warning might have cut the response time—but that would have been risky because of the human monitors. Still, in a real emergency—

The coach slowed and stopped. They stepped out into a monstrous natural cave that Henrys was sure did not show on the survey maps. It was dry, but there was the smell of the sea about it. They must have pumped it out, gaining a hideout no outsider would suspect. Too much of a job for fugitives operating without power equipment; the sheer weight of the sea would have balked them. So it must have been prepared before the Conquest.

There was no electric power here now. The risk of exposure was not great if they generated their own electricity—but the fields associated with that current could still be picked up by sophisticated detectors if a thorough search were made. And the massive generators would be extremely difficult to conceal while in operation. So—no power.

The Ukes gave him a torch. They were sure of him now; obviously any attempt to escape would be futile. They walked in a line through the portals of the cavern. Henrys studied the rocky configurations in passing, looking for whatever might be of help to him—when the time came. Was there a weak spot where a sledgehammer blow might break through and let in the sea? Or could the ceiling of a passage be collapsed, blocking pursuit?

Was there a distant sound behind? Pfo was smart—but it would be foolish to stake his life on help from that quarter now.

An artificial wall appeared, with a portal inset. It resembled an air-lock, or a bulkhead against water intrusion. They screwed this open, passed into a tight chamber, and finally transferred through the inner lock into the lighted and heated interior. It *was* an air-lock— so the air inside would be free of the gaseous pacifying drug.

Armed guards clustered near. It would be impossible to infiltrate this fortress.

They passed through a minor maze of passages, then came to the polished inner court. It was a palace. The floors were not carpeted, of course, and there were no hangings on the walls to interfere with suction. But it was bright and clean and well illuminated by gas lamps set in artistic niches, and there were many of the trapezoidal vertical columns that the Ukes considered decorative. Walls of books were prevalent, and many of the partitions were of colored glass. This was business and residential comfort.

Henrys was conducted immediately to the throne room. The monarch was there: an old Uke whose green skin was wrinkled and whose suckers were faded. Unfamiliar with court etiquette, Henrys made a small formal bow. "I see you are well, King Brf."

"You have been granted your desire, alien," Brf said. "Why have you chosen to intrude?"

"I tried thinking like an entrenched, nonrepresentative, corrupt government," Henrys said.

A guard made a threatening motion toward him, but the king halted that with an unconcerned twitch of the elbow. "It seems you are apt at that."

"I realized that the system Earth and Kazo instituted could only be subverted if one of the parties cheated at the outset," Henrys continued, privately dismayed at Brf's nonchalance. "By pretending to relinquish control of the homeworld—"

King Brf quivered his tentacles in the Uke equivalent of a conscious yawn. "When an enemy fleet holds the planet hostage?"

"That fleet is unlikely to strike so long as its own people hold nominal control. Perhaps there are ways to put it out of commission. A lot is possible to a functioning government-in-exile." He paused momentarily, wondering how to strike fire. "But of course your scheme won't work."

"You appear to be effectively isolated," Brf said. "Yet we are disinclined to provide you with the secrets of our power. We shall not deny you the consolation of believing that our project is futile."

He was gaining no ground at all in this verbal engagement. The king simply would not be baited. "I find it hard to believe that you can hold out against your entire warren-net of trained fighters and saboteurs. You must have resources that are not evident."

"Strange—I was thinking the same thing about you. Your venture here seems foolhardy, and is not typical of your prior performance in office."

"When I discover your resources," Henrys said, "you may discover mine."

"A courteous but useless offer."

King Brf was obviously adept at bluffing, and was giving away absolutely nothing. Henrys knew himself to be overmatched, but still he had to try. "I'm not sure you properly appreciate the threat, King. The warren-chiefs, feeling betrayed, will report what they know to the Conqueror government. The humans will in turn institute a rather thorough search-and-destroy pattern, utilizing the most sophisticated devices. Then, with a combined Earth-Uke siege on your suckers—"

"Your conjecture becomes dull," Brf said. "I suggest you estimate the maximum time this theoretical chain of events will require, and note the passage of the hours.

When that maximum has expired, you will know you were in error." He rotated both elbows. "Confine the alien without duress," he ordered.

How certain Brf was. Not even any interrogation! He seemed to be indifferent to the very real threat Henrys had outlined. Was he deranged—or was there superior logic behind his attitude? If the latter—why hadn't he at least deflated Henrys' own bluff by describing his plan for victory? Surely the human government *would* locate this hideout now, and soon dismantle it.

Henrys walked with the guards to the small cell prepared for him. It was well appointed with a lamp, water, sanitary facilities, and even several Uke books.

He settled down on the bunk. They must have expected him, for Ukes did not use beds; they slept suspended from some convenient elevation, like Earthly possums. This was disconcerting also; it reminded him of Bitool's confidence in dealing with an armed assassin. King Brf had to be dealing from strength.

The books were genuine, too. He unfolded one, making out the characters with fair facility. He had worked hard to master the language and culture of Uke, but probably would never be completely comfortable in them. This was a semi-philosophical text covering one of the obscure intellectual disciplines of the planet.

There was also folded blank plastic paper together with the tiny writing quills the Ukes used. Henrys' fingers were clumsy compared to their facial tentacles, but he could make do.

> Dear Serena,
> I am at present suffering the excellent hospitality of the late King Brf, former monarch of Uke and a subtle individual. He has seen fit neither to execute me nor to use me. Strange whim!
> The reasonable man adapts himself to the world, according to *The Revolutionist's Handbook*. The unreasonable one persists in trying

to adapt the world to himself. Therefore all progress depends on the unreasonable man.

I am, as you know, unreasonable. What alarms me is my suspicion that the king is less reasonable than I.

What secret can be at once so potent that it means certain victory for the Uke monarchy— yet so vulnerable that one alien prisoner cannot be permitted to know it?

And there it was! Conversation with Serena had produced the proper question after his own mind had failed. Find a scheme that could be undone, potentially, by a lone captive—

A guard came to the gate. "Now?" he inquired in English.

Henrys had schooled himself not to do double takes. No Uke was supposed to know any language of Earth. This had to be the Kazo spy Nuxto, who had somehow infiltrated into this stronghold. "No," he murmured, not lifting his eyes from the letter.

The spy moved on. This was Henrys' ace—that unexpected factor that Brf had guarded against by his caution in giving away information. If mere knowledge sufficed to interfere with the king's plan, Nuxto could have used it. But as it was, Henrys remained helpless, and it was pointless to give away the spy's identity for nothing.

Back to thought: if Brf had no concern about Conqueror investigation, it had to be because the king's plan would take effect before the human government could act. Atomic technology made such swiftness possible—but obviously Brf didn't have it here. Earth's detectors would have located any such machinery long since. So what was left? A biological bomb?

That mysterious nerve complex, and the inexplicable lapses in Uke history, and the term mngh . . .

Then it fell into place.

CHAPTER

11

◆ ◆ ◆

Henrys put away the unfinished letter. "Guard!"

A guard came. "What do you wish?" he asked in Ukish. It was not the Kazo.

Henrys grasped for his best course. It would be safest for him to wait until the Kazo inquired again, for the spy would choose an appropriate time when no natives were near. But that could be too late. He had to move rapidly.

"Inform your king that I know his secret."

"What secret?"

"The secret of conquest. He will understand."

The guard moved an elbow and departed.

In a moment he was back. Efficient communication! "Now?" English.

The Kazo had been alert, moving in the moment the guard left. "I have it—but I need to get word outside—at least to the revolutionist Pfo. Before Brf can act. This thing is potent. Humans may have to evacuate."

"The king is currently in his harem. The guard may not be able to reach him quickly. Tell me the secret; I will get word out."

"Not so fast, friend," Henrys said warily. "I'm not entirely sure of your identity—" The Kazo pulled off a sucker to reveal a blue three-fingered hand. *"Or* your loyalty," Henrys finished. "Help me escape."

The Kazo worked the devious locking mechanism and opened the gate. "What do you require?"

"Take my place. Stall the king as long as possible. Then use whatever weapon you have and make your break. You can hide among them in a way I cannot—especially since they'll be looking desperately for *me!* How did you get in?"

"I followed you, then merged with Twe's party. I was on the pedals at the end of the coach. But that risk is nothing compared to what you ask. Is it worth it?"

"I'll talk while you change. Deal?"

"You are trusting!"

"The Ukes have a nerve complex that is normally inactive but is vital for species survival. When war or tyranny or other calamity threatens the welfare of the species as a whole, a telepathic linkage occurs that unites every native within range and imposes one supreme command: eliminate the threat. Everything else is blanked off, and death has no meaning—so long as that threat exists. Afterward, no one remembers. They call it mngh—the inexplicable. An involuntary species reflex, a blanking out—but it does the job."

The Kazo was already changing. His suckers came off and his limbs extended to approximate those of a human being. He was well trained; Henrys knew an ordinary Kazo would require many hours to accomplish what he was doing in minutes. No doubt these talents were variable, as were those of humans; proper exercise could make a man capable of feats of strength far beyond the ordinary, and proper discipline could—but that was irrelevant. Of course the spy would be expert. His life depended on it.

"King Brf must have discovered a way to control that reflex," Henrys continued hurriedly. "To invoke it—and suppress it. Otherwise it would have been triggered by the Earth 'conquest' of Uke. We would have faced mass madness when we landed, complete indifference to the threat of planetary incineration—instead of the conventional reaction we got. Uke science has been advancing exponentially in recent decades, just the way Earth's and Kazo's have. They must have been fascinated by the same mysteries of history and biology I noted—and had far better opportunity to explore them."

"Why *not* invoke it at the time of conquest?" Nuxto asked. Now he was applying makeup to his skin, converting from green to white, and accepting Henrys' clothes as he stepped out of them. The face-tentacle mask lay on the floor with the suction gloves. A skilled impersonation!

"Because it would only have got the planet blasted from space," Henrys said. "A biological imperative is useless at a range of fifty thousand miles. They had to mix with us, get their menials aboard our ships and their leaders on our worlds—they already control *yours,* you know!"

"I know," the Kazo said grimly. "But they've behaved so far, because of the remaining human Conquerors." His face and hands became human now, as he put on five-finger gloves, ears, nose. He had obviously made this transformation before, but the change was amazing.

"So now the king will exercise his power and trigger that reflex. It won't matter what the natives were doing before, or which side they're on. This supersedes it. Every Uke will drive mindlessly to exterminate the threat—which is obviously the alien presence on the planet—after which King Brf will resurface. Normal history will resume after another inexplicable mngh lapse. Or so I conjecture."

"That explains much," the Kazo admitted. "But how does he start it?"

"Maybe you can find out," Henrys said. "If we knew that, we might stop it." He studied the other. "You aren't a perfect ringer for me. You're too short, and your face is sallow—"

"Have you looked at yourself recently?"

Henrys spread his hands—and the Kazo imitated him, practicing mannerisms. "You know best. You certainly do look human, and probably all men look pretty much alike to them. Now I'll hide, and you can—"

"What a pretty scene—two men!" a voice said in Ukish. It was King Brf. "But I think we had better—"

The gate was open. Henrys launched himself through it at the king and his four guards. They were armed—but with primitive weapons. Two pikes came down to meet him.

But they had underestimated the human reaction time and acceleration, that was much superior to sucker movement. Henrys grabbed the descending spears and hauled on them. Useless; he had once again forgotten that sucker anchorage! While he wrestled for control, the other two guards came at him.

A heat beam crackled by Henrys' head and seared the facial tentacles of one attacker. The Kazo had a modern weapon! Henrys let go the spears and clubbed his fist into the torso of another guard. The Uke emitted a ghastly croak and collapsed. Their bodies were extremely vulnerable to hard punches.

The king half turned. Henrys knew he was going to call for help. But two guards remained between him and Brf. "Stop him!" Henrys hissed.

The Kazo had already perceived the danger. The heat beam sounded again, the lightning of its passage making the air explode in small thunder. Steam puffed out from the king's face and he fell, silently.

Henrys whirled on the guards, expecting a berserk attack. But they seemed stunned by the disaster. For the moment they were leaderless, without direction.

"Damn!" the Kazo said in English. "I'm afraid I killed him. Aiming through these bars—"

"Couldn't be helped," Henrys said, though he was sorry too. Brf had been an exceedingly clever Uke, even going to the trouble of setting a trap for the Kazo spy. A trap that had been sprung. The king had outsmarted the two aliens neatly—except for that beamer. Henrys saw now that the weapon was plastic: transparent to the metal detectors of the Ukes, so he could carry it anywhere. Henrys himself had not anticipated the weapon, so he hadn't outsmarted Brf. He had just been luckier.

"This could trigger that mngh," Nuxto said.

"No. Kings have died before without historical blanks.

And no one knows it yet, except these two guards. He must've ordered everyone else away, so as not to expose the secret we were working out."

"He needn't have worried," Nuxto said. "Which of them would have understood it—in English? He doesn't strike me as all that smart."

"We could have yelled it out in Ukish anytime. Though why it should be kept secret from his own guards—"

"It can't be something just within one mind. Brf could not have suppressed the reflex in eleven billion natives as the alien ships came down. His nervous system would have burned out. But it could be that a *group* of minds—"

"Such as the king himself and a troop of guards!" Henrys exclaimed. "Yes, it would have to be kept secret, or it could spread like fire and be out of control. Probably he has amplification of some sort, that either triggers it simultaneously all over the planet, or suppresses it. An artificial telepathic field—"

"That requires electronics," Nuxto reminded him.

"It could be set up elsewhere on the planet, with only the controls here. Or technicians waiting for a signal—"

"We're wasting time," the Kazo said. He was already changing again. "We'll have to cover up what we've done, so we can discover the rest of Brf's secret and stop the signal, or whatever it is. Otherwise we haven't accomplished a thing!"

Henrys agreed. He herded the two guards into the cell and locked them in, then stood guard himself at the main tunnel-entrance. How lucky they were that the Ukes were not truly telepathic, and that electronic communications did not exist in this refuge. They had a fighting chance to complete their mission.

"Prop him up," the Kazo said. "I'm better at Ukes than at humans—but this will be extreme."

Henrys propped the king up. The beam had vaporized his left eye and probably penetrated to the brain, killing him. The wound has dribbling green ichor that obscured the lower features. Henrys felt sick; he reacted violently when threatened, but the killing of any sentient creature was appalling to him despite his position in the court. This was close and real and tangible—and Brf had been more than sentient.

The Kazo's white face shaped into the Uke configuration. He erased the man-color, applied green, and donned the tentacle-mask. He kicked off Henrys' shoes and put on the suckers. Henrys saw that they were not mere stick-ons; the three flexible toes of the Kazo fitted into special slots and operated little valves to make the suction work. But of course he could not match the natural performance of the natives, and stayed off the walls lest his clumsiness be obvious. How the mask worked Henrys could not imagine. The Kazo had fooled natives before; could he now actually emulate the old king successfully?

"Now his robes," Nuxto said, stripping off Henrys' clothing. Henrys pulled the royal apparel from the corpse. The king was wizened, and parts of his skin were bleached into an unhealthy white.

"One thing," Henrys said. "I doubt that he could walk ceilings anymore. His muscles are weak, and his suckers brittle. So you won't have to—"

"But his mind remained sharp. I heard his dialogue with you. Let's see if I can match it." The Kazo donned the robes, made finishing touches, struck a pose, and switched to Ukish: "You have been granted your desire, alien. You shall be reduced to serf status, as will all your kind."

Henrys was startled. "Letter-perfect!" he exclaimed. "He didn't actually threaten me with serfdom, but if I had not seen you change—"

"I'll keep it conservative," Nuxto said. "These Ukes must know their king well. I cannot fool them long."

"You'll do better if we arrange a distraction. I'll be your prisoner—you'll take me to the throne room for private interrogation. They'll be watching me more than you, because I'm so obviously alien. Maybe we can find the secret before they get suspicious. But we'll have to get rid of the body, and silence these guards."

"I also have a stunner," the Kazo said. "It will knock

them out for two to four hours. We can tell the others you tried to escape, using that—"

"Oh-oh," Henrys said, looking at the prisoners. "Something strange about them."

The two Ukes were stumbling about aimlessly in the cell, clutching their heads. They banged into walls and gate but did not seem to notice. One climbed the wall, but dropped off, then climbed again.

"Are they in pain?" Nuxto asked. "I have not seen such behavior before."

"The opposite," Henrys said. "They seem numb. What's ailing them?"

"They have seen what we are doing. If they understood enough—"

"Good God!" Henrys exclaimed. "We must seem like a real threat to their species survival, and we killed their king. It's the reflex!"

"But what they're doing is purposeless!"

"It's just started—and they're confined. Must take a while to warm up—and they don't have anything concrete to orient on yet. But it'll spread—and we'll be in the middle."

"Then we've triggered it ourselves," Nuxto said. "All we can do is run and hide, before they overwhelm us."

"No!" Henrys cried. "This thing'll spread like cancer across the planet. It'll wipe out everything—and our cake system along with it. We *can't* escape! We have to stop it, somehow. We're the only ones who can."

Nuxto considered. "You're right. Once it starts, it must spread planetwide within hours. But Brf's equipment must be able to damp it out—and he must have had some shelter for himself, so it wouldn't have *him* dropping off walls." He glanced meaningfully at the prisoners.

"So now we know our immediate mission," Henrys said. "We can't be sure it's reversible once it really gets going, but we've got to try. The sooner we find that secret, the better our chances. And just in case it hasn't spread yet, you'd better beam those two into unconsciousness now."

"Yes," Nuxto said, doing it. "Meanwhile, get yourself out of sight, or you may trigger it all over again. I'll tackle the damping on my own. The moment they find out the king is dead, someone will start that amplifier going, and then we really will be sunk. But if I can fool them long enough, maybe you can escape and carry word to the government, and they can shut down all power planet-wide and perhaps stop the action long enough to locate the equipment. That gives us two chances to stop it."

"Chances are still less than even, I think," Henrys said. "Maybe I can still create a diversion—"

"Just get out! If they're berserking, we don't need any diversion. If they aren't, you could trigger it again."

"You're right! Fine spy I'd make! But I'm still not satisfied. If that was mngh, they still lacked orientation. That must come separately—maybe from the dominant personality among them. Like the king. So—"

"There'll be a new king soon! Get moving!"

Henrys retained his doubt, but couldn't formulate it. "All right. I'll get out. If I can."

He had a rough idea of the layout of this region, and headed through the tunnels for the air-lock-exit. Probably he'd have trouble with the guards—but if they weren't anticipating trouble . . .

Still his mind mulled over the problem. There was too much he didn't understand about the Uke trance-state. Perhaps it could be controlled—but that would have been a very recent development. Through virtually all of the history of the species, it had to have been natural—and it could *still* be natural. Maybe no actual amplification was required.

He reached the main portal, having eluded stray palace personnel. It was well guarded, and he had no weapon. The guards did not appear to be suffering the mngh. One or two he might overcome by a surprise rush; three or four he might set back long enough to scramble through the port and slam it shut. But there were six.

He backed off, concealed within the dark tunnel. He had indulged in more than enough hazardous heroics already. It wasn't just his own life he was risking, but the future of three worlds. And he still wasn't sure he had the real answer to the riddle of mngh. It was the family trait of the Henrys: to act, then reconsider, then become uncertain . . . but sometimes that chain connected to something significant.

A natural trance-state—yet it had not spread to the guards of the gate. Could such a seemingly slow process abruptly be converted to a controlled, artificial state? Or would it be necessary to make use of the natural propensities, perhaps only modifying the thrust of the trance? He was getting nowhere.

Henrys turned back. Escape would be difficult—and possibly disastrous. Let Nuxto think the human had got away cleanly; in the event of the Kazo's capture the Ukes would not be able to gain true information from him. Henrys could continue to investigate quietly on his own. If the Kazo succeeded in locating and disarming the mngh apparatus, nothing was lost. But if Henrys' growing reservations were correct, he might yet have to unriddle it himself.

Or was he merely becoming muddle-brained from fatigue?

A darkness loomed. It was the body of a Uke, blocking the light penetrating the passage entrance. One of the guards had spotted him.

Henrys scuttled back. It was a mistake, for he tripped and fell. "Halt!" the guard cried, standing on the ceiling. "Indentify yourself."

Hardly! Henrys found an offshoot and tumbled down it. He was in trouble now. If he had just waited it out—

More guards were coming. He knew they would be circling about, blocking off the available exits. There weren't many tunnels here, for this was no labyrinth, just an undeveloped section of the hideout. They should not know about Brf's death yet, because of the Kazo's impersonation—but by this time they had to be aware that the human prisoner was at large. He was unlikely to remain that way long.

Still he fled, hunched over, driven by that increasing uncertainty. If he found a passage big enough for him to stand upright, he could outrun them and perhaps evade the immediate net. Then, maybe—

The tunnel curved upward, steeply. No problem for a Uke—but disaster for him! He tried to mount it, but could not; his feet skidded and his hands found no grip on the smooth sucker-polished surface. He dodged back.

And collided with a guard. The Uke, whose reflexes were keyed to its own kind, had not anticipated the fugitive's sudden reversal. Henrys knocked him aside and charged on.

He tried an alternate tunnel that he had bypassed before. He couldn't continue making mistakes indefinitely; he had to choose correctly at least once! This one led to a larger one, where he could at least run freely. He did so.

There was better light here, emanating from holes in the ceiling. Apartments, he decided; in a confined region like this, every passage went somewhere. A Uke in an Earth apartment house would be similarly confused.

Three more Ukes appeared around a curve. "RRWR!" Henrys bawled, setting them back in fright. Then he was upon them, punching one, shouldering another, and kicking the third. His atack was devastating because of their susceptibility to hard blows on the torso. He scooped up one of their weapons—a needle-shrapnel sling suitable for puncturing sucker pads—and charged on.

He had improved his position by dint of sheer brute strength. The Ukes could no longer be certain they had him contained, or which side of their net he was on. Their search pattern would become patternless. But he would have to take proper advantage of his gain, or he would lose what little initiative remained to him. He had to use his elbow-room to solve the riddle of the mngh trance.

Where would the secret be hidden, assuming any external evidence existed? He had thought the throne room —but perhaps that was too obvious, and of course the Kazo was checking it out. If not there, where? Surely close by, for the king's convenient access. Secret passage? Hard to manage with a constant royal entourage. How could the king go there freely, yet with proper privacy?

The royal bathroom? No, menials would have to service it, and there would be no secrets from them.

A business office? No—too many functionaries would pass through.

Then he had it. The harem!

All kings had harems, overtly or covertly. According to Nuxto, the king had been there just before getting Henrys' message. It would be death for any male underling to intrude.

But how to reach the harem? It should have an entrance from the throne room or nearby, and be well guarded. If he couldn't navigate the main gate, he certainly couldn't sneak into the harem. He might need the Kazo's help after all.

He turned another corner. The tunnel debouched into a room—and it was filled with Ukes!

Henrys tried to stop, but stumbled into the room. The Ukes turned. Something ugly manifested. There was no outcry, but a kind of joint loathing. They milled about; then one stepped toward him, unsteadily. The others followed.

The mngh! These palace attendants were reacting the way the guards in the cell had—but now there was no barrier between them and the alien.

He ran, with the silent mob in pursuit. He ducked through another portal—and skidded directly into the throne room.

Nuxto was there, regally ensconced. He looked exactly like King Brf. "So you have given yourself up, alien!" he said. "I had expected more of you."

It was so like the late king that it made Henrys nervous. Of course the act had to be good, to fool the Ukes; how much easier to fool an Earthman! Even if Brf had survived the burn, he would have been blind in one eye; this king had two unscarred, functioning eyes.

The mngh crowd surged through the doorway. Guards

leaped to contain it with crossed pikes. Surprisingly, this was effective; the maddened Ukes desisted.

If the mngh were abroad, why were the guards sane? The effect seemed highly selective. And why did the pursuers allow themselves to be so readily balked? That attitude hardly represented a serious threat to the human government.

"I shall interrogate this creature privately," Nuxto said.

"Majesty—" an official protested.

The Kazo dismissed the objection with a neat twirl of his elbow, only the slightest of jerks betraying the alien inadequacy of joint. "If this human possessed the means to harm me, he would have used it from ambush. Obviously he is beaten. The mngh slavers for red blood, as he has discovered." He stood. "Follow, Conqueror!" he said with a beautifully sarcastic flair.

Henrys followed meekly. Nuxto was overplaying the part—but was carrying it off nicely.

"Throne's a blank," Nuxto murmured in English as they walked through a polished back passage. "I found the sanitary facilities, harem, some sort of jail, and a tiger cage—but no secret exits and no equipment. I didn't dare *ask* . . ."

"I've got a lead," Henrys replied. "Harem."

"Oh? I *wondered* what the old rogue wanted with a pretty young Ukulele!"

The expression bothered Henrys as unnecessarily crude, but this was no time to debate etiquette. "Why aren't the guards affected by the mngh?"

"Not sure. But I noticed scars; I think they've been operated on. Had their nerve severed."

Of course! The king and his personal guard, plus those at key points like the main gate! Cut that nerve, and the mngh would be lobotomized. An obvious precaution.

But something bothered him. A seeming inconsistency he couldn't quite place. . . .

There was a roar. They passed a room-sized cage set

into one side of the passage, containing a monster. A rrwr.

"Watch this," Nuxto said. He slid a gate across the hall behind them, almost flush with the near wall of the cage. They went on by, the rrwr pacing them hungrily, its huge suckers fastening to the trapezoidal bars without a slip. At the other end of the cage he pulled another gate into place, using his own suckers with admirable finesse. That section of the passage now resembled a thin oblong cage beside the larger one.

Then the Kazo pulled on a wheel. Disks for suckers projected from it like the spokes of a ship's control. A system of gears disappeared into floor and ceiling. As they turned, the barred front of the cage moved out into the hall, slowly. The entire piece was on runners, attached to reduction gears.

In a moment the rrwr's cage had expanded by the width of the passage. There was no way out except through the cage—which was no way out.

"Only possible to work it from this end," Nuxto said. "Glad I figured that out. Complete privacy—no one bothered old Brf when he came here."

"I wish I'd had a better chance to know him," Henrys said. "I rather like his mode."

"He was our enemy," the Kazo reminded him. "Why should he give up his dream of a three-planet empire for us? He was too smart to let live!"

"The last time I heard that reasoning," Henrys said slowly, "it applied to a Kazo. An overlord of Earth."

"The trouble with you, human, is you believe too naïvely in the basic decency of sentient nature."

Henrys sighed. "Yes. It is dangerous to be sincere unless you are also stupid. That's from the handbook of a mythical revolutionist of Earth, John Tanner. But it is a danger I feel obliged to take."

"You are *not* stupid," Nuxto said as they walked on.

"No? That depends on viewpoint. Do you know I love a Kazo female?"

"Intellectually, you mean. That's possible."

"As a member of the family."

"Well, wait till you see the harem! Maybe you'll love a female Uke."

Henrys laughed shortly, though he found it not at all humorous. The Kazo was impertinent.

Now they were at the jail. Half a dozen Uke males lay sprawled in as many cells.

"They've been drugged," Henrys said, something important clicking at last. "Ukes never lose sucker control like that in normal circumstances—not even when unconscious."

"Odd," Nuxto murmured. "They can't get out—both bars and rrwr contain them. Why drug them also?"

"Because they're sensitives!" Henrys cried. "Ukes whose minds trigger off the mngh-state in others! Brf kept them drugged so that they could *not* set it off!"

"You mean I passed right by these, looking for a machine . . . but they can't be the only sensitives on the planet."

"They may be, for the moment. I believe Brf sought out all the others and killed them, just before the Earth-conquest materialized. Perhaps one person in every thousand. In time new ones will mature—but for now this is it. Now that he needs them, he's letting them recover."

"Yes—I see that now," Nuxto said. "That must be why the effect is so slow to develop. They're still groggy, and their sensitizing and broadcasting nerves aren't functioning properly. But in a few hours they'll be ready to go among the natives—"

"And mngh will spread at full intensity, unstoppable," Henrys finished. "I don't know what the range of a sensitive is; maybe the effect is self-sustaining, like a forest fire."

"So now we know the mechanism," Nuxto said.

"Yes—but not its control. That's vital."

"Control—of a state of *un*control?"

"Establishment must be distinct from direction," Henrys said carefully, working it out in his own mind. "If the mngh is to serve its purpose of species salvation. Otherwise it could be abused—as it is being abused now, for the first time in Uke history."

"Abused? Why shouldn't the Ukes make use of it to promote their power—if they can?"

Henrys looked at him. A minority suspicion suddenly became majority. He had an explanation why the guards accompanying the king to Henrys' prison cell had gone mngh, and so could not have been operated on. "Because in this case it is being used *against* species interest. The cake system will spare the Ukes the one threat the mngh cannot abate: the collapse of their civilization owing to overpopulation and depletion of resources. If the mngh is perverted to oppose the cake, the species will perish— and perhaps two other species with it."

"Really—if you were a Uke, would you accept that thesis?"

"I have felt it was a mistake to conceal the nature of the cake from the individual populaces," Henrys said. "Now I am sure of it. An uninformed Uke *cannot* accept my thesis."

"I doubt that an informed one could, either."

Henrys smiled, gaining confidence. "There lies our difference. We're about to put it to the test."

CHAPTER
12

They arrived at the final chamber of the tour: a richly appointed Uke apartment. "The king's harem," the other said mockingly.

There was only one female in it. She was very young, barely nubile by Uke definition. Far short of the ideal sex object, he was sure.

She looked up and saw Henrys. "Oh!" she said in her language, frightened. "What is it?"

"Let me handle this," the supposed monarch murmured in English. Then, in Ukish: "Vne, this is a sentient from another planet, Earth. His name is Henrys. He comes to talk, not harm."

"Sire," she responded respectfully. "Must I meet him? I am afraid, and I am not feeling well. . . ."

English: "Must she?"

"Yes," Henrys said firmly.

"My dear, the alien's concern is extremely important. I know you are not feeling well, but you must deal with him."

"Sire," she said, sadly acquiescing.

"First I must ascertain what you know," Henrys said. "May I make myself comfortable? I know my aspect disturbs you, and you need not look at me."

"Yes . . . yes," she whispered, facing away. "Sire,

will you stay with me? Only with you do I feel safe. . . ."

"Of course, my dear." He put one sucker gently to her light green head in a Uke gesture of comfort.

"Do you know of my kind?" Henrys asked.

"No. Not before this meeting," she said faintly.

"Do you know of any other world? Kazo?"

"No."

"Then I must tell you a great deal," Henrys said. She had been kept in complete ignorance, and now he knew why. In quick summary he described the conquest of Uke by the forces of Earth, the ongoing reduction of population, and other policies recently instituted.

"Can this horrible thing be true?" she asked, her delicate elbows fluttering.

Again the sucker reassured her. "Yes, Vne."

"I feel so ill. . . ."

Henrys was sure she did. She was responding to the increasing intensity of the emanations of the sensitives, just as the mngh mob in the main palace was. But he had to proceed. "This is only part of the story, Vne. The part most Ukes have been told. But this conquest is apparent, not real." And he described the cake analogy and its political application.

"I do not understand," she said.

"It is not necessary to understand, right now," Henrys said. "Just assimilate the facts, and remember. Perhaps I should explain your own role in this—"

But she seemed suddenly much worse. Her slender body shuddered, her mouth tentacles writhed, her suckers lost their purchase, and her breathing was uneven. "Please," she said plaintively. "Please, let me hide. . . ."

The Uke face looked at Henrys over her bowed head. "There is no hiding from this, Vne." Then, to Henrys, in English: "I believe it will take a few minutes, and we do not know the outcome. Perhaps we should settle our own business in the interim."

Henrys nodded. "I am armed, of course. So are you. Wouldn't it be better to wait on her?"

"Your illustrious father, Admiral Henrys, once met a

Kazo spy in human guise. He suspected from the outset, but did not challenge until he was sure—and then he chose to negotiate. In that caution lay the future of the man."

"You appear to know more about the matter than I do," Henrys remarked.

"I make it my business to keep track of counterrevolutionists," the other said.

"But are the situations analogous?"

"I suspect they are. You understand why I spared you."

"Because you always keep your important options open," Henrys said. "That is also why you set up this counter-government, and arranged to control the mngh. If the humans cheated—"

"You did not use your shrapnel sling, once you knew."

"Had I been certain you were evil, King Brf, I would have used it," Henrys said. "But when a pattern emerges—"

"And, like your father, you prefer diplomacy to violence."

"Like him, I am prone to violence. And subsequent regret that disposes me to greater caution the second time. I'm sorry your double died."

"He did not die. He will be blind, but I shall care for him well for the service rendered. May I inquire what gave him away?"

"His mngh-susceptible guards."

"Ah, well. Your Kazo accomplice is unharmed. Things did fall out rather conveniently."

Henrys laughed, releasing tension. "King, with your talent for improvisation—you certainly could not have anticipated all these events, yet you adaped them to your purpose as though they were elements of a firm master plan."

"That is the genius of my office," Brf said. "But you were always the key, Richard Henrys. A man with the mind to divine and the courage to act, yet the caution to ascertain the complete truth before performing the irrevocable."

"That is my impression of you," Henrys said. "So it seems my mission was superfluous."

"On the contrary. I view you as Bitool did."

Henrys was no longer surprised by Brf's knowledge. The king had gone to the considerable trouble to master English and become thoroughly conversant with the politics of the cake, so that he might acquit himself effectively in a situation such as this. No ignorant or obtuse tyrant, this! "Bitool had larger information than that available to me at the time."

"Precisely," Brf agreed, twirling his elbows with that trace stiffness of age. "Now we shall listen to Vne. She was never my concubine; it was for this moment I preserved her, naturally."

The Uke maiden had changed. She rose from her illnesses of body and spirit like a radiant flower from humis. There was now a queenly aura about her.

"He who invokes mngh knows not the nature of its thrust," Vne said. "I will hear your petitions now."

King Brf spoke first. "I ask for abolition of the alien presence on Uke, and extension of my empire to the worlds of Earth and Kazo."

It was Henrys' turn. "I ask that there be no interference with the unique exchange of governments we have arranged, so that these three worlds and perhaps others can be saved from their natural extravagances and thus survive."

Vne turned to King Brf. "Your ambition is flawed."

He bowed his head. "I feared it was."

She faced Henrys. "Yours, too, is imperfect."

He looked up, dismayed. "What?"

"Yet there are necessary elements in each," she said. "As an interim measure whose framework is already functioning, your cake must serve. The new empire shall be fashioned on that base."

Both Brf and Henrys stared at her. "*Both* empire and cake?" Henrys asked. "They are mutually exclusive!"

"Summon the Kazo," Vne said. "Quickly."

"This is ludicrous!" Henrys cried. "The mngh is intensifying! That's why you have been awakened. There will be planetwide slaughter—"

But Vne would not respond. She stood still, possessed of her special splendor even in repose.

"There is reason," Brf said. "She is the controller—the only one alive. She will have her way—or there will be disaster. The mngh must be guided!"

"But to what purpose—"

"Patience, young alien! I understand the order no more than you—but the mngh is never capricious. We must act at once. Come with me."

They hurried back down the hall. The prisoned sensitives were now recovered from their drugged state—but were themselves victims of the mngh. They wandered aimlessly. "So long as they live, mngh continues," Brf explained briefly. "At the moment Vne withholds control, but that can't last long. Mngh must be controlled—or it will be uncontrolled. I spent many years locating every sensitive. Otherwise the alien landing or some other catastrophe would have triggered it. . . ."

"What if some other controller has matured since you went underground?" Henrys asked.

"That is one danger. Control based on partial or erroneous information—"

"Yes, I see," Henrys said as they came up to the rrwr cage. "Lucky we got the truth to Vne in time!"

"A king does not leave such matters to chance," Brf said. "I would have drugged the sensitives again, had your actions not forced my sucker. In any event, I planned to acquaint her with the truth when the time came. But without a living alien as proof, I might not have convinced her: another danger." He worked the gate-wheel, seeming less old and worn now that he wasn't imitating himself. "You must remain here, closing the passage after me. The safety of our educated controller is of paramount importance. Preserve her as you would your Kazo love."

Low shot! "But the undirected mngh out there—" Henrys protested. "Can you fetch Nuxto safely?"

"Not safely—but I can fetch him. Be ready for my return, for the mngh does not answer to my authority."

The hall was open, the rrwr pushed grudgingly back. King Brf hurried on through.

Henrys watched the rrwr, and it watched him, as he turned the gear-wheel to close off the passage. The dragon looked as if it weighed about a thousand pounds, lean. Its facial feelers were like the tentacles of a small squid, six to eight inches long: no doubt superlative for holding struggling prey to the sharp tusks and great trapezoidal teeth. There were slender spikes along its sinuous flanks, that sprang out at right angles when it snarled. It would be hard to strike that monster in any vulnerable place.

"Alien."

Startled, he discovered little Vne behind him. "You should not be here, Controller," he said. "There may be violence."

She put a sucker through the bars. The rrwr flattened its ears—it had none, but that was the impression—and backed away, somehow aware of her power. "There will be violence," she affirmed. "All over this world, Ukes shall kill Ukes. It shall be a horror such as the species has not known—and shall not know again."

"What of the humans?" he asked apprehensively.

"They shall be spared."

"Then you are supporting the cake!"

"*And* the empire. When this night is over, the unfit natives will be gone. The population will be two billion. The aliens will not need to kill anymore, and will be able to ease their discipline accordingly. Uke will be a full member."

"The mngh can do that?" he asked, amazed. "I thought—"

"Mngh polices its own. Any problem the mind of one native can grasp, mngh can resolve," she said. "You have shown mngh what is necessary."

Henrys shook his head. "Such carnage! It's hard to believe."

"Mngh is not belief. Mngh is power."

He looked at her again, so small yet regal. "Still, you have come to the alien for something."

Her majesty wavered momentarily. "When mngh is over, and I revert, you must send me to planet Kazo."

Henrys considered. Vne's natural self was hardly the type to be chosen for that select service. But on Uke she would be marked; too many nerve-severed natives would remember her role in the mngh. In past centuries no Uke had avoided the trance, so there were no recriminations; but that had changed. There would be no place for her here; the blood of billions would be on her suckers, however necessarily. So her request was reasonable.

And if the entire ugly job of selective population control was accomplished in one night, freeing human hands and conscience of that monstrous burden, protective exile for Vne would be quite in order.

"All right," he said, knowing his government would cooperate once the truth was known.

She walked back to her apartment while he remained at the gate. How glad he was that the rrwr was securely caged —and that it stood between him and the developing mayhem.

He heard a sound in the distant tunnels—a massive bellowing. The invisible ears of the rrwr pricked forward. Henrys put his hands on the wheel, nudging the barred wall just a bit.

The noise became louder. Henrys moved the wheel again. It balked.

Oh-oh. He shoved it around harder. The give was minimal. Something was jamming it.

Then he saw what the rrwr was doing. The creature stood facing him, two suckers firmly planted on the floor against the sliding barrier, blocking it.

Coincidence—or design?

The rrwr eyed him and made a "rrrwwrr" that sounded like a chuckle.

Two figures came into sight beyond the cage. Brf and Nuxto!

Henrys yanked at the wheel. The barrier strained at the

blocks, but could not budge them. The bellowing amplified.

"Open!" Brf called urgently in English. "They're too far gone to listen to me anymore. My guards are holding them back for a while, but—"

"The animal is blocking the gate!" Henrys yelled.

Brf looked. "He never did that before!"

"Maybe you never starved him like this before."

Ukes charged down the passage. No guards restrained them now. They were obviously crazed, chasing anything that fled.

Henrys brought out his shrapnel sling. The needles would perforate the rrwr's suckers and lame it, freeing the barrier.

"No!" Brf cried. "Mngh is the greater threat! We'll go through the cage!" And he opened the gate.

Henrys had to desist, knowing that a wounded rrwr would be even worse than a balky one. What a predicament—all to honor the whim of Vne!

The rrwr moved. In one sinuous bound it was at the open gate; in another it was through. It knocked Brf and Nuxto aside and plunged down the passage to intercept the mob, spiraling up the wall and across the ceiling as it went. Had it overlooked the immediate bait—or did it hold some little affection for the king, its familiar keeper?

Henrys watched, fascinated, as monster met maddened Ukes. The rrwr's mouth-tentacles clasped a native and threw him under its back—for it was on the ceiling now —while its body spines held off the others. Then it grabbed another and and bit off his arm with one motion. The rrwr's motive was plain: it was famished, and it had suddenly been confronted by unlimited prey.

Yet that seeming cunning, blocking the barrier—how smart *was* it? Had the wild creature patiently waited its opportunity to escape? Ordinarily such a ploy would not have worked, as it could have been drugged. But this time, with the ravening crowd coming and the king on the wrong side . . .

Brf and Nuxto were through. "I think that rrwr's

smarter than you figured," Henrys said as he closed the gate behind them. "Maybe some of the mngh affected it—"

"It would have been smarter yet to stay caged," Brf panted. He was old and unused to such exertion. "I left the other gate open so it could fight in the larger space— but *this* gate we must seal!" And he unhooked a large Uke lock, passing it through the bars to make a secure closure.

For a moment more they watched the fray. The tide of battle was already turning. The rrwr could not maneuver with full effect in the narrow hall, and the Ukes seemed oblivious to pain or injury. Now the mngh had a temporary object, and it concentrated mindlessly upon it. But this, too, was limited by the passage; only two or three Ukes could come to grips with the rrwr at one time.

Nevertheless, the mass of the crowd was forcing the rrwr back, slowly. Ukes set themselves on floor, wall, and ceiling, clinging to the animal wherever a handsucker could find purchase. When it stepped back to gain room, they pressed forward. The rrwr fought viciously, beginning to realize that the relationship was no longer predator-prey, but life against life. The mighty teeth crunched body after body, and corpses were accumulating underneath, forcing further retreat. Green blood actually flowed down the incline of the passage toward the cage. But still they came.

Henrys tried to imagine an Earthman with a blaster substituting for the rrwr. The outcome would be similar; one weapon could not keep firing indefinitely. Yes, the mngh was power!

"On!" Brf said. He led the way to Vne's apartment. Henrys, though fascinated by the gruesome battle, turned and followed.

"Is there any other exit?" Nuxto asked anxiously. He still looked like a Uke, but patches of white and even natural blue showed through his clothing.

"None," Brf said. "This is our safest refuge. We are seeing in microcosm what all the world experiences."

Henrys hoped that microcosm didn't wipe them out.

There seemed to be little selectivity to the mngh so far.

They reentered the apartment. Vne was there, composed. "The empire and the cake are imperfect, separately," she said, as though there had been no interruption. "Together they can form a workable larger system. But you will have to fashion it yourselves. Uke, Earth, and Kazo—a committee of three."

"I suspect I have missed something," Nuxto murmured.

Vne ignored him. "You three, representatives of your species, shall institute an interworld committee to oversee the operations of the cake. When the time comes to abandon that system—and that shall be within this decade—you shall institute the empire proper. In this way you will preserve your worlds from the larger threat."

The three spoke together. "Larger threat?" Brf demanded. "How can we trust—" Nuxto started. "We have no authority—" Henrys said.

They stopped. What was the point in debate? If what she said made sense, something of the sort would develop. If not, there would be time later to reconsider.

"We must choose committee members we can trust absolutely," Brf said. "I know a number of Ukes—"

"No," Vne said firmly. "Each new member shall be selected by agreement of the existing members of the two other species. You three select the first round only; later six will select, and on, as far as necessary."

"The cake system after all!" Henrys exclaimed. "Always the separation of interest—"

There was a banging noise down the hall. "I must proceed," Vne said. "Alert me if personal danger manifests." She retreated into her quiet trance.

"That must be an attack on the near gate," Henrys said. "The mngh has overcome the rrwr."

"Then we'd better get down there and defend that gate," Nuxto said, pulling off his suckers and mask. "If the rrwr couldn't hold them back—"

They hurried toward the noise. The dragon was not down, after all, but it was fading. The Ukes were massed in the cage, hemming it in, driving at it constantly, clinging like leeches despite the punishing spikes. Bodies littered the floor, and there was a slime of green throughout. Many of them had sucker weapons: hard balls for throwing, needle daggers for stabbing. The rrwr was bleeding from a score of cuts, and was now very tired. It did not know how to deal with this awful persistence that knew no pain or fear or common sense.

Brf's elbows sagged and his tentacles quivered. "Such an ignoble end to such a noble beast!"

Several Ukes were working on the inner gate, with little science but much determination. They were hammering at it with fragments of stone. The bars were beginning to rattle.

Henrys sized up the tactical situation. "We don't want to use our regular weapons until we have to; there are too many of them. But if we can get clubs, we can defend this gate."

Brf went to an alcove and brought out bright metal rods. He had anticipated such defensive needs long ago.

Nuxto shucked what remained of his Uke uniform, limbered his blue fingers, and twined them about one rod. Brf fastened a sucker to the flat end of another. Henrys tucked a reserve rod into his belt. They commenced knocking suckers.

"About the committee nominations," Nuxto said as he caught two suckers with one vertical blow between bars. "That young revolutionist Pfo impresses me. I overheard some of your conversations."

"I guess I'm the other non-Uke," Henrys said. "I certainly don't object to that selection. And I'll nominate the Kazo female Serena, if that isn't too cozy." He bashed a sucker on his own.

"She is a suitable choice," Brf said. "It *is* cozy, she being your adopted sister—but by the same token we know her values. I shall nominate the human Jonathan Teller."

"Jon!" Henrys exclaimed.

"I don't know that name," Nuxto said.

"A childhood friend of Henrys'," Brf explained.

"Spared from extermination by the intercession of Bitool because he was the son of a Conqueror. It was a standard policy that led me to suspect the motives of those governments—but it had some fortunate results. Conqueror Teller now serves on planet Uke, and has an excellent record. He is in charge of counterespionage and has given my agents extreme difficulty—not least by his assignment of Henrys to this case."

"That's good enough," the Kazo agreed.

The mngh Ukes were becoming more aggressive as they oriented on this new center of resistance. So many suckers were gripping the bars, and so many others hammering, that it was impossible to keep them all off. The din was terrific. "I hate to say this," Henrys shouted, "but we're stacking the committee with my friends. Aren't you afraid of bloc voting?"

"We must choose from those we know best," Brf pointed out. "Will any of your friends compromise for the sake of that friendship?"

"Of course not!" Henrys said. Now he was using his clubs, banging suckers and arms and occasionally heads as though playing on drums. "They're—"

Then he was stopped by a noise from behind, barely audible over this clamor, but significant. He whirled to look—and saw more Ukes. "The sensitives!" he cried. "They've broken out!"

"I should have fixed that defective lock!" Brf cried. "They must be caged again. If they kill the controller—"

Henrys now had some notion what that would mean. "But if *we* kill *them,* the mngh will stop."

"Mngh must run its course!" Brf replied. "Vne is even now organizing it planetwide with sane direction. Soon it will function as it should. She will terminate it when it is time."

They left the weakening gate and approached the sensitives warily. Four were free; two had not yet been released. The four no longer wandered aimlessly. They recognized the aliens and charged.

Henrys hefted his club. Could he knock them out without killing them? Or would the mngh keep them fighting so long as life remained?

The first reached him, suckers aiming for some hold on his face. Henrys' eye still smarted from the time Smy had done that, and he dodged aside quickly. He caught the creature about the rubbery waist and lifted him before the foot-suckers could anchor on the floor. He threw him over his shoulder and carried him to the first cell. He dumped the Uke and slammed the gate closed.

The gate-clasp was broken. He could not lock it.

Behind him the attack on the rrwr-gate intensified. Without its defenders it would soon be breached. But the sensitives had to be dealt with first! If he left *this* gate, his prisoner would immediately escape!

An arm reached over his shoulder from behind, adhering to one of the bars. Henrys shoved back, trying to get away, but this Uke's feet were anchored to the floor. The pre-mngh stage of sucker incontinence was past. If he could just wrestle this one into the cell, he might have two of the four caught—but how could he budge those suckers?

He stomped on them. The hard heel of his shoe crunched into the leathery top of one sucker, and it came loose. He tromped the other, then lifted and hurled. The sensitive crashed into the gate. Henrys jerked it open and half rolled, half carried the Uke through. He backed out and slammed the gate again. Two down!

Nuxto was on the floor under the other two sensitives. Henrys had to go to his rescue—but still couldn't leave the gate! Where was Brf? Dead—or fled?

The rrwr's gate crashed open. The mass of wild Ukes jammed through.

Now it was every sentient for himself! Henrys let go of his gate and jumped into the adjacent cell, shutting himself in. This lock was also broken, but he might be able to hold out for a time.

Then he realized: he had to protect the controller! He had made one of his typical pressure-blunders, putting himself out of the fray. Now the throng was upon him.

Suckers reached through the bars, some holding green-bloody stones. Henrys shoved open the gate and charged out, hoping to surprise the savage crowd, but the mngh was immune to surprise also. The weight of many bodies bore down on him, suckers reaching from floor, walls, and ceiling. He kicked and punched desperately, but it was hopeless. The mngh might be capable of doing the job of planetary population control, but Richard Henrys had just thrown that chance away. Neither man nor Kazo would emerge from this pit to set up any committees!

The Ukes paused. They stood as if frozen in thought, eyes half-closed. Then they marched as one, back down the hall to the rrwr cage, and through it, and away, funneling neatly into single-file formation and tramping carelessly over the bodies of their former mngh comrades. The sensitives were of that number, now indistinguishable; even the last two had been freed from confinement.

Henrys got up, battered. Nuxto was unconscious, but he lived, and no blue blood actually flowed.

What had happened? Was it over already?

One old Uke appeared from the other direction. Henrys jumped—but it was King Brf! "Personal danger manifested," he remarked sanguinely. "So I alerted Vne. The time we made for her was enough. She is in control now, and was able to divert a small local effort. . . ." He walked on, stepping daintily over the splattered green. "I hope my poor rrwr survives."

Henrys shook his head dazedly. He could not imagine how the mngh would selectively prune away over eighty percent of its own membership, but he was suddenly very sure it would do so.

After this night of carnage, the new era would begin.

All Sphere Books are available at your bookshop or
newsagent, or can be ordered from the following address:
Sphere Books, Cash Sales Department,
P.O. Box 11, Falmouth, Cornwall.

Please send cheque or postal order (no currency), and allow
18p for the first book plus 8p per copy for each additional
book ordered up to a maximum charge of 66p in U.K.

Customers in Eire and B.F.P.O. please allow 18p for the first
book plus 8p per copy for the next 6 books, thereafter 3p
per book.

Overseas customers please allow 20p for the first book and
10p per copy for each additional book.